"I know he's _____ _____ ___ here he's just one of us."

"I know that," his cell mate, Tim Kerry, said. "I just don't know who he's aligned with."

"He ain't been here long enough to join with anybody. And there might be some folks in here who wanna kill him as much as we do."

"That's what I mean," Kerry said. "Let's find out who we got backin' us before we make a move on somebody like him."

"Okay, okay," Barton said, "maybe you're right, but I'm gonna promise you this. Clint Adams ain't gonna walk out of Yuma Prison alive."

DON'T MISS THESE
ALL-ACTION WESTERN SERIES
FROM THE BERKLEY PUBLISHING GROUP

THE GUNSMITH by J. R. Roberts
Clint Adams was a legend among lawmen, outlaws, and ladies. They called him . . . the Gunsmith.

LONGARM by Tabor Evans
The popular long-running series about Deputy U.S. Marshal Custis Long—his life, his loves, his fight for justice.

SLOCUM by Jake Logan
Today's longest-running action Western. John Slocum rides a deadly trail of hot blood and cold steel.

BUSHWHACKERS by B. J. Lanagan
An action-packed series by the creators of Longarm! The rousing adventures of the most brutal gang of cutthroats ever assembled—Quantrill's Raiders.

DIAMONDBACK by Guy Brewer
Dex Yancey is Diamondback, a Southern gentleman turned con man when his brother cheats him out of the family fortune. Ladies love him. Gamblers hate him. But nobody pulls one over on Dex . . .

WILDGUN by Jack Hanson
The blazing adventures of mountain man Will Barlow—from the creators of Longarm!

TEXAS TRACKER by Tom Calhoun
J.T. Law: the most relentless—and dangerous—manhunter in all Texas. Where sheriffs and posses fail, he's the best man to bring in the most vicious outlaws—for a price.

FOURTEEN

It was the next morning, at breakfast, when Clint saw the women.

He had found himself sitting at the same table with the same prisoners as the night before. When he saw the three women come in, he leaned over to the man sitting beside him.

"There are women here?" he asked.

"Just those three."

"I didn't know they put women in Yuma Prison," Clint commented.

"Not that many," the man said. "You gonna eat that?"

Clint looked down at the mess in his plate that was supposed to be eggs.

"No," he said, "I'm just going to have the biscuit."

"You mind?"

"Help yourself."

Since they were keeping their voices down, none of the other men at the table realized what was going on until all of Clint's eggs were on the other man's plate.

"Thanks," the man said. "My name's Cates, Jack Cates."

"Clint Adams."

Cates nodded. He was a big, hulking man with shaggy blond hair and beard stubble.

"I know who you are," Cates said. "You're gonna have ta watch yer back."

"I always do."

"No, I mean, really watch yer back in here," Cates said. "The word's gone out on who you are. And you ain't got no gun in here."

"I see what you mean," Clint said. "Thanks for the warning. Tell me about the women."

"Don't know much," Cates said. "Don't know what they're in fer. The guards usually keep them for themselves."

"You mean . . ."

"Yeah, they pass 'em around," Cates said. "The women get treated pretty well as long as they cooperate with the guards and give 'em what they want."

Clint saw what Cates meant. The women seemed to get different food, not the mess the men were eating, and they got a table for themselves, away from the rest of the prisoners. Two of them looked to have black hair, one red. They were wearing dresses that matched the pattern on the men's shirts and trousers, but their clothes looked clean, as did their hair. Well, if what Cates said was true and the guards were using the women for sex, they'd want them to smell like women, not like prisoners.

Clint went back to eating his biscuit. If he didn't want to be constantly hungry, he was going to have to learn how to eat the slop the prisoners were served for their meals.

He looked over at the women, who seemed to have not only eggs, but meat. Many of the other prisoners were looking at them as well, either because they were eating better food or simply because they were women.

As Clint watched, one of the dark-haired women looked over at him and caught his eye. There was a moment of recognition between them, but he was convinced it was on her side, not his. Even when she looked away, he stared at her, but became convinced he didn't know her. That meant she must have recognized him from somewhere.

He leaned toward Cates again and asked, "How many other prisoners get special favors?"

"Only a couple," Cates said. "If you got money and power on the outside, you can get special treatment on the inside."

"Can you steer me towards them?"

"Sure, why not?" Cates asked. "After all, you gave me yer eggs, right?"

FIFTEEN

PRESCOTT, ARIZONA

EARLIER

He still had hours before the meeting at the Tin Pot Saloon. He decided to find the place while it was still light out and take a look it.

It turned out the Tin Pot was a small saloon on the side street, in an area of town that appeared to need some rehabilitation. There were empty storefronts on either side, and just a few stores across the street that were still open.

When Clint entered the Tin Pot, the first thing that hit him was the smell, the second the cramped quarters. This certainly did not seem the kind of place a woman would come to.

The place smelled like a bunch of ranch hands had just come in off the range without cleaning up first. Clint looked around, expecting to see cow manure on the floor.

"Beer?" the bartender called.

Clint waved his hand at the man and backed out of the place. The smell was too much for him. There was no way he could have stood in there and had a beer. He decided to walk around the building, see how many other doors there were.

Several minutes later he had determined there was only one other door to the saloon, in the back. He'd return later for the meeting.

Clint decided to go and see the sheriff, fill him in on his meetings with the chief and the mayor. He felt that the sheriff was a kindred spirit. Maybe if he spent more time with him, the man might come forward with the truth, because as much as the man might be a remnant of the Old West, he was still lying, too.

Clint entered the sheriff's office, found the man seated behind his desk.

"Hey, Adams," Coyle said. "Pot of coffee on top of that stove. How about fillin' two cups?"

"Sure."

Clint found two tin cups next to the stove, filled them with coffee, carried them to the desk. He handed the lawman one, then sat down with the other one.

"In case you're wonderin'," Coyle said, "I was just waitin' for somebody to come in so they could get me a cup of coffee. You're the lucky one."

"No problem."

"What's on yer mind?"

Clint decided to be frank.

"I talked with the mayor and the chief."

"And?"

"They each lied to me."

"So? That's what politicians do. Was that a surprise to you?"

"No," Clint said, "I figure everybody in this town has lied to me about Harlan Banks."

"Why do you think they done that?"

"They're hiding something."

"The whole town?"

"The people I've talked to."

"Then," Sheriff Coyle said, "why don't you talk to some more? Maybe you'll find somebody who won't lie to ya."

"What about you?"

"Whataya mean?"

"Well, you've been lying to me."

"What makes you say that?" He seemed totally unconcerned about having been called a liar.

"Come on, Sheriff," Clint said. "I know Harlan Banks was here in town. He sent me a telegram from here. Obviously he got himself into trouble and something happened to him. That couldn't have all happened without you knowing it."

"Why not?"

"You're the law."

"I used to be the law," Coyle said. "Now the police department is the law. If you think somebody knows something they're not telling you, go to the chief."

"As I said, I already talked to the chief. He told me to leave town tomorrow."

"And the mayor?"

"Him, too."

"So you'll be leavin' tomorrow?"

"Maybe."

"I thought you said—"

"Never mind," Clint said. He leaned forward, set the coffee cup on the desk, and stood up. "I've got things to do the rest of the day."

"Adams," Coyle said, "why don't you just do what you're told and leave?"

"I can't do that," Clint said.

"I can't help you, you know," Coyle said. "Even if I wanted to, I can't."

"Actually," Clint said, "I believe that if it comes right down to it, you'll do your job."

Coyle put his own cup on the desk and said, "Don't bet your life on that, Adams."

SIXTEEN

Clint left the sheriff's office, still not convinced that Coyle would stand by and do nothing if Clint was in trouble. But as the man had suggested, he certainly wasn't going to bet his life on it.

He had two options while waiting for his meeting at the Tin Pot. He could go to his room and wait there, accomplishing nothing. Or he could go to Hannah's Café and . . . do what? Have more pie? A steak? Or maybe he had more options. Like a saloon and a few beers.

Then a thought occurred to him. He could go to the livery stable, check on Eclipse, and talk to Handy. Even if he was related to the sheriff, maybe he'd have something to tell him about Harlan Banks.

He found Handy mucking out some stalls at the livery.

"Not takin' him out of here already, are you?" Handy asked, leaning on his pitchfork.

"No, not yet," Clint said. "Just wanted to check in with him."

"That animal eats more than any other two horses," Handy said.

"Yes, he has a good appetite."

Clint walked to Eclipse's stall, stroked the big horse's neck, spoke to him briefly while Handy continued his work.

"Hey, Handy," he said, coming out of Eclipse's stall.

"Yep?"

"I found out something interesting."

"What's that?"

"You and the sheriff are apparently cousins?"

Handy stopped mucking, sniffed, and said, "Yeah, our mothers was sisters."

"You're not happy about that?"

"We might be related," Handy said, "but we ain't exactly friends."

"Well, that's too bad."

Handy leaned on his pitchfork and stared at Clint.

"You got somethin' on your mind, my friend," he said. "I ain't the smartest guy in the world—like my cousin keeps tellin' me—but I know that. Is there somethin' you wanna know about the sheriff?"

"No," Clint said, "there's something I want to know about Harlan Banks."

Handy lifted the pitchfork up and drove it down into the ground two or three times.

"What'd my cousin say?"

"He never heard of him."

The pitchfork went up and back down.

"You talk to anybody else in town?"

"Lots of people," Clint said. "They're all lying to me. I know Banks was here, he sent a telegram from here, and then he disappeared."

"You talk to the chief of police?"

"The chief, and the mayor," Clint said. "They lied to me, too."

"Lots of people lyin' to ya."

"That's the way it looks."

"So why ya askin' me?"

"I was thinking maybe you were different," Clint said. "I thought maybe I'd get the truth out of you."

The pitchfork went up then down again.

"I tell you what," Handy said. "This here's the truth. If I was you, I'd just forget all about this Banks fella and get out of town."

SEVENTEEN

Clint didn't push Handy. After his meeting at the Tin Pot, if it yielded nothing, maybe he'd go back and try applying some pressure. Handy didn't like his cousin, the sheriff, but he was also careful. Another man who was from a bygone time.

He decided to go to Hannah's to kill the time until the meeting. When he entered, only one table was taken, and Hannah was waiting on the man herself. Ben was nowhere to be seen.

"Mr. Adams," she said, facing him with a coffeepot in her hand. "Just the man I want to see."

"Oh? Why?"

"Coffee while we talk?"

"If it comes with a piece of pie."

"Peach?"

"Of course."

"Have a seat."

She went into the kitchen, came out with a slice of

peach pie and a fresh pot of coffee. There was already a cup on Clint's table. She filled it, put the pie in front of him, then sat across from him. It was his first good look at her face. She was a pretty woman, but did nothing to enhance it. She was a hard worker, probably concerned only with paying her bills and raising her son. Beneath her apron was a womanly, almost matronly figure. Nothing unattractive about that, at all.

She stared at him with frank and very brown eyes.

"What have you got my son into?"

"What do you mean?"

"You know what I mean," she said. "He's so excited to be helpin' the famous Gunsmith. So what have you got him into?"

"Nothing much," Clint said. "He's asking some questions for me."

"The kind of questions that will get him hurt?"

"I doubt it."

"The kind of questions that will keep him from his job here?"

"He said no."

"I see."

Clint looked around.

"Doesn't look busy. Maybe he'll be back for the rush."

"The rush is over, and he was here," she said.

"Then there's no problem, is there?"

"Maybe not," she said. "Maybe that remains to be seen."

She looked over at her other customer, who seemed to be finishing up.

"Let me take care of this customer," she said. "Enjoy your pie."

"I will."

She stood up, walked to the other table, and settled up with the gentleman, who seemed very satisfied with his meal.

"Everybody seems to leave here happy," Clint said when she came back.

"Is that so?"

"Seems to be the case."

"What about you?"

"I leave happy every time."

She stared at him, a new look in her eyes. She was appraising him, measuring him.

"You know," she said, rubbing her palms along her hips, "I work very hard."

"I'm sure you do."

"I have a lot of stress."

"You're running a business," he said. "Comes with the territory."

"I don't get very many opportunities to . . . relax."

"Does Ben live with you?"

"He does, and it's a small house."

"What about here?"

"He's usually here all the time," she said, "but tonight he's not."

She reached behind her to untie the apron and let it fall to the ground. The dress she wore beneath it was cheap, the material thin, and it clung to her, showing off her hips and breasts. She wasn't making any secret what she had on her mind.

"What do you say, Mr. Adams?" she asked. "Want to help me relax? No obligations afterward?"

"I think we better lock the door."

"I think so, too."

She walked to the door, closed it, locked it, and pulled the shade. Then she pulled the shades down over the other windows. She turned to face him and shrugged off her dress. He stood up, staring at her. Her breasts were pendulous, with large brown nipples and aureoles. Her hips were wide, thighs almost chunky. She was not built to be a saloon girl in a gown, but her body was perfect to be naked in a man's bed.

EIGHTEEN

He approached her as she stood, almost shyly, with her hands behind her. He touched her, immediately raising gooseflesh on her.

"This is bold of me," she said. "Don't think badly of me."

"I won't," he said. "I promise. But what if Ben comes back?"

"The door's locked, and he doesn't have his key," she said. "He'll go home."

"Well, then . . ." he said.

He pulled her to him and kissed her. Her body was hot; the smell of her was a heady combination of sweat, food, and her own natural scent. She opened her mouth to him and they kissed avidly. He slid his hands down her bare back to her buttocks, then gripped her tightly and pulled her to him even more. She moaned into his mouth and her hands grabbed for his belt.

"Wait," he said. "Here?"

"Right here," she gasped. "I can't wait."

He removed his gun belt, set it down nearby, where he could get to it. He let her undo the belt of his trousers, then the buttons, and yank them down to his ankles. He lifted his feet so she could pull off his boots, and then remove his pants and underwear completely.

His hard cock stood up and poked at her. Her eyes widened as she took it in her hands and stroked it lovingly.

"Oh, my," she said.

"Oh, yes," he said. He pushed her back until her butt struck a table, which she then sat on. He spread her legs, stood between them, and kissed her mouth, her neck, her shoulders, and her breasts. When he took a nipple into his mouth and sucked it, she gasped and grabbed his head, holding him there.

He switched to the other breast, sucked it hungrily. Her breasts were solid, the skin smooth. And her nipples were a delightful mouthful.

He continued to kiss her, down over her abdomen and her belly, until he had his nose and mouth buried in her pubic hair.

"My God," she said, "what—" She stopped short when his tongue darted out and touched her. "Oh!"

He began to lick her avidly, and she grew wetter and wetter, both from him and from her own emissions. She groaned and began to rock as he sucked and licked her. The table jumped noisily, and threatened to break beneath her weight.

"Oh, God," she gasped, "don't stop . . ."

* * *

Ben entered the Hotel Kellogg and approached the front desk. His friend, Larry Kellogg, whose father owned the hotel, was working the desk.

"Hey, Ben," Larry said. "How are ya?"

"Good, Larry, good," Ben said. "Listen, I been askin' around to see if this feller was a guest in any of the hotels a few weeks ago."

"What fella?"

"His name's Harlan Banks."

Larry's face immediately reflected his recognition of the name.

"Geez, Ben, what are ya askin' about that for?"

"I'm askin' for a friend of mine," Ben said, "whose name happens to be Clint Adams."

Larry's eyes went wide and he said, "The Gunsmith?"

"That's right."

"And he's your friend?"

"Sure he is."

"And he's lookin' for this fella, Banks?"

"Yep."

"Why?"

"I don't care why," Ben said. "I'm just tryin' to help him out. So?"

"So . . ."

"Come on, Larry," Ben said. "The way you're actin', I know the man had a room here."

Ben reached for the register. Larry made a half-hearted attempt to stop him, but Ben opened the book and saw that a page had been torn out.

"Larry . . ."

He turned the book around so Larry could see.

"Ben, look," Larry said, "my dad said not to say nothin' . . ."

"And who told your dad not to say anythin'?"

"Well, he's on the town council," Larry said. "So it musta been the mayor."

"But why?"

"I dunno," Larry said. "Pa just does what the mayor tells 'im to do."

"Yeah, I know," Ben said. "A lot of people do."

"Not your ma," Larry pointed out. "She pretty much does what she wants ta do."

"I know," Ben said. "Ma's a strong woman."

"Yeah," Larry said sadly, "my pa ain't like that."

"Okay, so," Ben said, to get back on the subject, "you remember this Banks fella?"

"Yeah, I do. He was—"

"You don't gotta tell me," Ben said, cutting him off. "Will you talk to Clint?"

"The Gunsmith?" Larry asked. "You want me to talk to the Gunsmith?"

"Yeah," Ben said. "I'll put the two of you together."

"Well, gee . . ."

"Larry? Come on, man."

"Yeah, okay," Larry said. "Okay. I'll talk to 'im."

"All right," Ben said. "You stay here and I'll go and get him."

"You know where he is?"

"I'll try his hotel," Ben said, "and then I'll see if maybe he went to the café. Just stay here 'til I get back, you hear?"

"I hear ya, Ben," Larry said, not sure he was doing the right thing. "I hear you."

NINETEEN

Clint lifted Hannah off the table, afraid it was going to break beneath her weight. It would certainly break under their combined weight.

"The kitchen," she said, hanging on to him, kissing his neck, wrapping her strong legs around him. "There's a table in the kitchen that's strong."

He nodded, took them both to the kitchen, which was hotter than the rest of the place because of the stove, even though it had been shut down for the night.

"There," she said, pointing.

He saw the table. Somebody had built it to be extra sturdy. He went over to it and set her down on it, spread her legs, and wasted no time. He drove himself into her and she gasped, her eyes going wide.

"Oh my God," she said very loudly, "it's been so long . . ."

She grabbed for him as he drove himself in and out of her, and before long the room was filled with their grunts, the smell of their combined perspiration, and the sound of their flesh slapping together . . .

Ben went to Clint's hotel, asked the desk clerk if he was there.

"I seen him go out, Ben," the man said. "Ain't seen him come back."

"Did he ask you about a man named Harlan Banks?"

"He did," the man said. "I don't know nothin' about that."

"Okay," Ben said. "When he comes back, tell him I'm lookin' for him. You know where I live?"

"I do."

"Then you tell 'im."

"I will."

Ben nodded, turned, and headed for the café.

Clint slid his hands beneath Hannah's butt, got both his hands full, and pulled her to him. She grunted every time they came together, their breathing coming in hard raps . . . and then there was a banging on the door.

They stopped.

Ben got to the café and tried the front door. It was locked, the shades were drawn, but the lights were still on. He figured his mother was inside, cleaning up. He put his hand in his pocket, but realized he didn't have his key.

He started pounding on the door.

"It's Ben," Clint said.

"Oh, God," Hannah said, clinging to him.

They remained that way for a moment, and then the banging started again,

And then they were laughing, trying not to laugh out loud.

"Shh, shh," she said, "we can't let him hear us."

"What if he keeps knocking?"

"He'll stop," she whispered. "He'll figure I left the lights on and he'll go home."

They stayed pressed together until the knocking stopped. They listened intently, hoping to hear footsteps walking away.

"He's leavin'," she said.

"Yeah."

She wiggled her hips.

"You're still hard inside me."

"And you're still gorgeous."

He kissed her, tentatively at first—in case the knocking started again—but then more avidly, and in no time, they were lunging at each other again . . .

Ben stopped knocking, tried to look underneath the drawn shades, but in the end he decided his mother must have forgotten to douse the lights. He'd have to go home, get his key, come back, and put them out.

He backed away, wondering where Clint might be. Maybe on the way home he'd stop in a few of the saloons and see if he was there. He was still hoping to get Clint together with Larry that night.

Ben finally walked away from the café, turning once to look over his shoulder. His mother hadn't left the lights on in a long time. He wondered what she had on her mind that made her do it this time.

TWENTY

Hannah pushed Clint away and got herself down off the table. Then she turned him around so she could get on her knees in front of him. He leaned back against the table as she took his hard cock in her hands, stroked it, cupped his balls, licked the shaft, and then took him into her mouth.

Clint groaned as she began to suck him, her lips sliding up and down him wetly.

"Mmm," she moaned as she sucked him. She ran her hands over his thighs, up over his belly and chest, and then around behind him to grab his ass and squeeze it.

"Jesus, Hannah," Clint said, putting his hands on her shoulders, then on her head as she bobbed up and down on him.

She started to make slurping noises, and he felt that if he didn't stop her now, it was going to be over before he was ready.

He reached down, slid his hands beneath her arms, and lifted her forcefully off his cock with an audible *pop.* He turned her, bent her over the table, spread her buttocks, and entered her from behind.

Hannah almost screamed, bent over so that she was lying flat on the table, her breasts flattened beneath her, as he drove in and out of her. She gasped and cried out with each thrust, and copious sweat was covering both their bodies.

Clint gripped Hannah's generous hips and continued to take her that way. He felt the buildup of his release in his legs first, and then he was spewing into her, roaring as he ejaculated in powerful streams.

Hannah felt the heat of his emission inside her, bit her bottom lip, but finally had to scream as she felt her own release push her over the edge . . .

Ben got back to the house he shared with his mother, found it dark. Annoyed, he entered and lit a lamp. It was obvious his mother had not been home. He wondered if he should go out and look for her, or keep looking for Clint Adams.

On the other hand, if he remained where he was, maybe one of them would show up there.

He decided to wait.

"Oh my God," Hannah said, catching her breath. She stood in the center of her kitchen, naked, and looked around.

"We didn't do any damage," Clint said. "I don't think."

"It's so hot in here," she said. "I'll open the back door to air it out."

Clint sniffed the room. She'd be airing out not only the heat, but also the smells of their lovemaking. It was probably a good idea.

"What will Ben do when he gets home and you're not there?" he asked.

"I know my boy," she said, opening the door. The breeze that came in immediately cooled the sweat on their bodies. Clint felt cold, but he couldn't get dressed until he had dried off. He doubted there was a bathtub anywhere in the building.

"I know what you're thinkin'," she said. "I have water, and cloths. I can bathe you."

"And he won't come back?" Clint asked. "And catch us?"

"No," she said. "He'll wait."

"Well . . . okay, then," he said, "but I get to bathe you, too."

"Don't you think that would defeat the whole purpose?"

He stared at her breasts, her nipples still distended, and said, "I'm sure it would."

He stood in the center of the kitchen while she dipped the cloth into a basin of water and washed the sweat from his body. When she got to his softening cock, it grew hard again as she dried it.

"Jeez," he said, gritting his teeth.

She washed his balls, his thighs, and his legs, then dried him off with another cloth.

"Oh my," she said, looking at his hard cock, "you're ready again so soon?"

"It's your fault," he said.

She laughed, then used the cloth and basin to clean herself. When she washed her breasts, and then her own crotch, his cock became even harder.

"If we don't get dressed pretty soon . . ." he said.

"Yes, I know," she said, and laughed.

They went back into the dining room to get dressed. As he pulled his clothes on, he watched her don her dress, felt a sense of loss when her lovely body was covered.

"Well," she said, "now what?"

"You better go and find your son, explain why he couldn't get in here."

"And you?"

"I have a meeting with somebody."

"To find the man you're lookin' for?"

"To find out about him, yes."

"Who are you meetin'?"

"I don't know."

"What if they mean to hurt you?"

"They probably do," Clint said. "I'll have to depend on myself to keep that from happening."

"You need help."

"There's nobody to help me."

"The law?"

Clint shook his head.

"They just want me to leave. I don't think they'd mind if I did that by getting myself killed."

"But . . . if you don't know who you're meeting, why go?"

"On the off chance they actually do have some information."

"Maybe Ben can help you—"

"No, I don't want to put him in danger. The only way he could help me is if he's already found something out."

"Well then," she said, "let's go ask him."

TWENTY-ONE

Yuma Territorial Prison

A few weeks later

The two guards were named Ace and Danny.

The girl's name was Amanda.

Ace and Danny had been guards at Yuma for the same six months. They had applied for the jobs and been hired at the same time.

Amanda had been an inmate for three months. She was inside for clubbing her bank manager boss over the head, nearly killing him, and stealing $40,000. The money was never recovered, but she was captured the next day by the local sheriff. She went to trial quickly, was convicted in record time of robbery and attempted murder and sentenced to ten years in Yuma. The bank manager was dead before the trial was over, killed by his wife when it came out in the testimony that he had been sleeping with his bookkeeper, Amanda King.

Ace was a big man, well over six feet, in his forties, with sloping shoulders, not muscular, but possessed of a rawboned strength not many men could match.

Danny was in his late thirties, shorter and slighter than Ace, but smarter. For a while they had been on the wrong side of the law, using Danny's brain and Ace's strength to pull jobs. But they got tired of running from the law, so they applied for jobs as guards in Yuma Prison, and wouldn't you know it, they got hired.

Amanda was a pretty woman, slender with pale skin and auburn hair. Men liked her, which was something she used to her advantage. In Yuma, however, the advantage always fell to the guards. But that didn't mean she—and the other women—couldn't use their femininity to get what they wanted, like warmer blankets and good food.

Some of the guards weren't bad when it came to sex. These two men, they always liked to take a woman together. Today, they had chosen Amanda.

They took her from her cell, walked her to a room the guards used. It had a bed, more comfortable than the cots that were in the cells. Sometimes they'd let her sleep awhile there afterward.

Today they pushed her into the room and Ace said, "Take off yer clothes."

It looked like he might be in charge today. If that was the case, this would not be easy. Ace was a brute. Sometimes Danny controlled him, and sometimes he let the big man have his way.

She undressed, folded her uniform, and put in on a chair in the corner. Naked, she faced them with her hands folded in front of her.

She had small breasts, but they were hard, like

peaches, with pink nipples. Ace licked his lips and undid his trousers. When he pulled them down, his cock sprang out, huge and pulsing.

Danny stood off to one side, still dressed. Sometimes he joined in right away, and some days he watched. Today he was going to watch for a while.

Ace approached Amanda, pawed her breasts, squeezing them, bruising them, biting them hard enough to break the skin on her tender nipples. She bit her own lip, so she wouldn't cry out. When he was done, he pushed her down to her knees.

"Open wide," he said happily.

She opened her mouth, and he thrust his penis between her full lips. She gagged when the tip hit the back of her throat, but then she began to suck him, working his cock in and out of her mouth, using her hands to further stimulate him. She knew she could get him to finish quickly if he let her. Sometimes he pushed her aside before he was done, but today he was carried away by the sensations of her lips, tongue, and hands, and before long he exploded into her mouth . . .

Clint had learned from Cates that the guards used the women for their own pleasure. He felt sorry for them, but he wasn't there to save them. He was there for a totally different reason, but maybe—if and when he got to see the warden—he could drop a bug in the man's ear. Of course, there was always the possibility that the warden already knew about it. Perhaps he was also part of it. Clint couldn't know that without speaking to one of the women, but so far—after a week in Yuma Prison—he still hadn't been able to do that.

In fact, after a week, he'd accomplished very little.

Danny dropped his pants, bent Amanda over the bed, and entered her from behind. Ace continued to paw her while Danny fucked her. She didn't mind Danny so much. Even erect, he had a small penis that she could accommodate with no problem. When Ace took her from behind, she felt like she was being torn up. It seemed like today she was just going to have to put up with a few bruises from the big guy, and not the usual abuse.

Danny grunted and groaned and emptied into her, then withdrew. Hopefully, they were done with her. But when she stood up and turned, she saw that Ace's cock was hard again.

"On your back, baby," he said, stroking himself. "Daddy's got somethin' for ya."

She obeyed, got down on her back, and opened her legs for him. As he drove his massive erection into her, she closed her eyes and tried to take herself somewhere else . . .

Amanda had heard that the Gunsmith was in Yuma. She had also been hearing talk about some of the prisoners wanting to kill him. She wondered how effective he would be as a killer without his gun. If they tried to kill him, and he managed to survive, maybe he was somebody she'd be able to use while he was in Yuma.

She had to think of a way to meet him, get to talk to him, maybe get to know him a little, and win him over to her side. With somebody like the Gunsmith on her side, maybe she wouldn't have to put up with the indignities heaped upon her by these guards anymore.

TWENTY-TWO

Clint and Hannah found Ben at the house, waiting for them.

"Hey," he said when they walked in, "I was lookin' for you two."

"I was looking for you," Clint said, "ran into your mother along the way. She offered to bring me here to see if you were here."

"I went to the café, Ma," he said. "You left the lights burning when you locked the door."

"I realized it later, dear," she said. "I went back and doused them."

"Why were you looking for me?" Clint asked.

"I found somebody you can talk to about Harlan Banks," Ben said.

"Who?"

"A desk clerk," he said. "He's a friend of mine. Banks stayed at his father's hotel, where he works."

"Well, let's go and talk to him," Clint said. "Maybe he can save me the bother of having to go to this meeting tonight."

Ben looked at his mother.

"Go ahead," she said. "I have to get myself washed up. When you're done, you can both come back here. I'll have a pot of coffee on."

"Sounds good to me," Clint said. "Lead the way, Ben."

Ben took Clint to Kellogg's hotel, found his friend Larry still behind the desk.

"Is your Dad around, Larry?" Ben asked.

"Naw, not tonight." Larry was staring at Clint with eyes as wide as saucers.

"Larry, this is my friend Clint Adams," Ben said. "Clint, this is Larry Kellogg."

"Hello, Larry."

"Muh—Muh—Mr. Adams."

"Relax, Larry," Clint said. "There's no need to be nervous. Understand?"

"Yuh-yuh-yes."

"Good," Clint said. "Ben tells me you know something about Harlan Banks."

"Um . . ." Larry said.

"Come on, Larry," Ben said. "Tell him what you told me."

"Uh, well, Mr. Banks did have a room here, but then he disappeared, and a page was torn out of our register."

"Who tore it out?"

"I don't know," Larry said, "but I figured it was my pa."

"And why would he do that?"

"My pa does what he's told."

"By who?"

"By the town council," Larry said, "or by the mayor."

"And the chief of police?"

"Him, too."

"And what about you? You don't do what you're told?" Clint asked.

"I do what my pa tells me to do," Larry said. "To the others, I'm nobody."

"Where's your pa now?"

"I dunno."

"Would he talk to me?"

"No," Larry said, "he'd be too scared."

"Okay, Larry," Clint said, "thanks for your help."

They turned to leave, but then Clint thought of another question.

"When Banks disappeared, did he leave anything behind in his room?"

"Nope," Larry said. "The room was clean."

"Who cleaned it?"

"I figured Mr. Banks took his stuff with him."

"What happens to stuff people leave in their rooms?"

"We got a room in the back," Larry said. "Pa keeps it for a while, then sells what he can."

"Can I see that room?"

Larry looked at Ben, who nodded.

"Okay," Larry said. "This way."

He led them down a long hallway to a back room, which was cluttered.

"Where would the newer stuff be?" Clint asked.

"Against that wall," Larry said, pointing.

Clint walked to the wall, looked at the saddlebags, weapons, books, clothes, carpetbags, and other things piled there.

"Nothing is marked with the room number they came out of?"

"No," Larry said.

Clint bent down, started to go through the saddlebags. There were clean and dirty shirts, bandannas, letters, and receipts. There were rifles laid against the wall but no pistols. The rifles looked as if they'd need to be cleaned after being there for so long, but one—a Winchester—looked newer, cleaner. He picked it up. There were two initials scrawled into the stock—small letters, but legible. "H.B."

"I'm going to take this," he said to Larry.

"Uh, okay."

"If your pa notices and wants to know where it is, tell him you don't know."

"Okay."

They left the room, walked back to the desk.

"Thanks, Larry."

"Yes, sir."

Ben nodded to his friend, and he and Clint walked outside.

"Is that Harlan Banks's rifle?" Ben asked.

"I think so," Clint said. "His initials are carved into the stock. Too much of a coincidence for it to be anyone else's."

"So now what?"

"Now I'll keep my appointment," Clint said. "See what else I can find out."

"Then what?"

"Then I'll have to come to a decision," Clint said. "Do I leave town, or do I press on?"

"If you stay, the mayor and the chief won't like it."

"Yes," Clint said. "I know."

TWENTY-THREE

They went back to the house, where Clint decided to leave the rifle, with Hannah's permission.

"I don't want it to be found in my room," he explained.

"We understand," Hannah said. "It's all right."

She served coffee for the three of them, and they sat at the kitchen table.

"When is your meeting?" she asked.

"About half an hour."

"Are you sure you don't want me to go with you?" Ben asked.

"Can you shoot a gun?"

"A rifle," Ben said. "I mean, I've been huntin'."

"Ever fire at a man?"

"No."

"Then you stay home, Ben," Clint said. "I'll be just fine."

"Are you sure?" Hannah asked.

"As sure as I can be," Clint said.

*   *   *

Clint approached the Tin Pot about ten minutes before
the time of the meeting. So far, it didn't seem as if Harlan Banks was such a secret that people were dying over
it. Whoever was behind his disappearance, they could
have killed Ben's friend Bobby for sending the telegram,
or Larry at the hotel for knowing that Banks had registered there. So maybe this actually was a meeting with
somebody who knew something, and not a setup to get
him killed.

He approached the batwing front doors of the small
saloon, and entered. This time when the smell hit him
he kept going.

"Beer?" the bartender asked.

Clint hesitated, then said, "Whiskey." He figured any
germs in the place would thrive in beer, but die in
whiskey.

There was four other customers, all sitting at tables
by themselves. Nobody was standing at the bar, so Clint
was alone there.

He sipped his whiskey and wondered which of the
four men had sent him the message. Two of them were
wearing holsters, while the other two were unarmed. It
didn't look like anyone was there to kill him.

"So?" the bartender said.

Clint turned his head and looked at the man.

"What?"

"You're lookin' for Harlan Banks?"

Now Clint turned his entire body to face the
bartender.

"You sent me the message?"

"Sure," the man said, "you don't think these other idiots can write, do ya?"

"What do you know about Harlan Banks?" Clint asked him.

"What's it worth to you?"

Clint studied the man for a moment. Did he actually have information, or was he just trying to cash in?

"That depends on what you've got," Clint said.

"Well . . ."

Clint took out some money and put it on the bar. The man looked at it, looked at Clint, waited, then took the money.

"That's a start," he said.

"Then tell me what you know."

"I know," the bartender said, wiping the bar top with a dirty rag, "I know where he is."

TWENTY-FOUR

Hannah found herself thinking about Clint, about what they had done together in her kitchen—on the kitchen table—and then, suddenly, she became aware that Ben was looking at her. She felt her face color, then she turned her head to hide the fact.

"What's wrong, Ma?" Ben asked.

"Nothin'," she said. "I was just wonderin' how Clint was doin'."

"Yeah, me, too," Ben said. "I think I shoulda gone with him."

"No, he was right," Hannah said. "You wouldn't have been of any help to him."

"I guess not," Ben said. "Still, if he gets killed—"

"He won't," she said.

"How do you know?"

"Because he's the Gunsmith, right?" she said. "This is how he lives his life. I assume he knows what he's doing in these situations."

"I suppose he does."

"So all we can do is wait," she said.

"Wait a minute," Clint said. "You know where Harlan Banks is?"

"I do."

"And you're going to tell me."

"For a price."

"How about this?" Clint asked. "You tell me so I won't shoot up this place."

"Go ahead," the bartender said. "If the word gets out that the Gunsmith shot up my place, I'll get more business."

He was probably right about that.

Clint took out some more money—more than before—and set it on the bar. The bartender looked at it, waited, but when no more was forthcoming, he picked it up and stuck it in his shirt pocket.

"So where is he?" Clint aside.

The bartender hesitated, wiped the bar some more, then said, "Harlan Banks is in Yuma Territorial Prison."

TWENTY-FIVE

"Yuma?"

"That's right."

"How long has he been in Yuma?"

"A few weeks, I guess."

"How did he get there?"

"He was railroaded in," the bartender said. "The chief of police, the mayor, the judge—"

"Judge?"

"Judge Fielder," the bartender said. "He's in the mayor's pocket."

"So the chief arrested him, and the mayor told the judge to sentence him to Yuma?"

"Now you got it."

"And how do you know this and nobody else I talked to does?"

"Because they held the trial right in here," the bartender said. "The Tin Pot courthouse."

"Why not City Hall?" Clint asked. "In a real court-room?"

"In a real courtroom they probably woulda felt they had to abide by the real law."

"So he was railroaded."

"Oh, yeah."

Clint finished his whiskey.

"You goin' in there after him?" the bartender asked.

"I don't know if I want to see him that bad," Clint said. "Thanks."

He turned and left the saloon.

After Clint left, the bartender called over one of his customers.

"Watch the bar 'til I get back."

"Sure thing."

The bartender—Tom Bennett—left the saloon and made his way across town to a residential area. He stopped at a large, two-story house and knocked on the door. It was answered by a gray-haired, middle-aged woman.

"Yes?"

"I need to see the mayor."

"You can see him at his office tomorrow."

"No," Bennett said, "he said he wanted to see me tonight."

"Come in." She let him in and closed the door. "Wait here."

She went into the house, came back ten minutes later.

"Follow me."

She led him to a study, where the mayor stood wearing a silk robe, smoking a large cigar and holding a brandy snifter.

"Tom," the mayor said. "This better be good."

"It is, sir," Bennett said. "The Gunsmith came to see me."

"And?"

"I told him that Banks was in Yuma Prison."

"And what did he say?"

"Not much," Bennett said. "I asked him if he wanted to go in there after him, and he said he didn't know if he wanted to see him that bad."

"Well," the mayor said, "if he wants to go into Yuma Prison, we can sure accommodate him."

"Yes, sir."

"All right, Tom," the mayor said. "Thank you."

"Sure thing."

"Let me know if he comes to talk to you again."

"I will."

"Maria will show you out."

Bennett turned, saw the woman waiting for him in the doorway. She showed him to the front door, and let him out. He started back across town.

Clint stood in the shadow of a house across the street. He watched the bartender go in, and then come out about twenty-five minutes later. A house that size, it had to belong to the either the mayor or the police chief. The bartender was reporting his conversation with him to one of them. Did that mean the information was false? Did they just want him to think Harlan Banks was in Yuma Prison?

There was only one way to find out.

* * *

He went back to Hannah and Ben's house. There was
no point in bracing the bartender again, because he
might still lie. And he doubted he was going to be able
to send a telegram from this town.

Hannah let him in with a sigh of relief, and Ben came
in from another room.

"What happened?" Ben asked.

"I've been told that Banks is in Yuma Prison."

"How did he get there?"

"He was apparently railroaded in," Clint said, "with
a quickie trial."

"So what are you gonna do?" Hannah asked.

"I'm leaving town tomorrow," he said, "to go to Yuma."

"Yuma?" Hannah said.

"The only way I'm going to find out if he's really in
prison is to go there and ask."

"How long will you be gone?" she asked.

"Well," he said, "if I find him, there won't be any
reason to come back here."

"My mom's peach pie?" Ben asked.

"Well, yeah," Clint said, "that would be a good
reason."

"Do you want some coffee?" Hannah asked.

"No," Clint said, "I think I'll go to my hotel and turn
in so I can get an early start tomorrow."

"Well, all right," Hannah said.

"Can you send us a telegram to let us know what
happened?" Ben asked.

Although he didn't know if he could trust the telegraph office in Prescott, he said, "Sure, I'll do that,
Ben."

He said good-bye to them at the front door, felt Hannah's grip on his hand tighten before she finally let him go. It had been a wild, enjoyable time in her kitchen that night, but he had more important things to worry about.

Like a man's life.

TWENTY-SIX

Yuma was a day's ride from Prescott. The prison was half a day's ride farther. He stopped in town to get himself a hotel room.

Yuma had been a major stop on the Colorado River until 1877, when the Southern Pacific Railroad built a bridge over it. So now there was only one steamboat company that utilized Yuma's port.

However, the prison provided a lot of jobs and commerce. As much as Prescott wanted to call itself a city, Yuma actually was one.

Clint was able to get a room in the Apple Blossom Hotel, even though the clerk told him the hotel was almost always full. Many people came to Yuma to visit their loved ones who were incarcerated in the prison.

"What brings you to our fair city?" the man asked as he handed Clint a key.

"Visiting the prison," Clint said, "but not to see a loved one."

Once he had his room, he went to the telegraph office and sent a telegram to Rick Hartman in Labyrinth, Texas. He wanted to know if Rick knew anybody in Yuma, or perhaps anyone who actually worked at the prison.

Clint went to a restaurant near the hotel for a steak, and while he was there, the telegraph operator came in looking for him.

"I have your reply, Mr. Adams," he said, handing it to Clint.

"Thanks very much."

The restaurant was filled with townspeople having their supper, and no one was paying him any attention until the key operator came in to find him. Now they were actually waiting for him to read his telegram. Instead, he set it down next to his plate, determined to leave it there until dessert.

After half an hour most of the diners who had seen him get the telegram had left the place. He finished his steak, ordered pie and coffee, and while he was waiting for dessert to come, he unfolded the telegram and read it.

There was only one person in Yuma that Rick knew and trusted. He gave Clint his name and told him how to find him. Clint finished his pie, paid his bill, put the telegram in his pocket, and left.

He entered the store, looked around, feeling comfortable. Once he'd wanted his own gunsmith shop. For a while he rode around the country in a wagon, plying his trade as a gunsmith. But soon the wagon became a burden, and it was his ability to use a gun that became important, not his ability to fix them, or build them.

But still, when he entered a gunsmith shop, he felt a sense of calm, as if he was at home.

"Can I help ya?"

He turned his head, looked at the man behind the glass counter. Beneath the glass were all kinds of guns, old and new.

"Ken Tohill?" he asked.

"That's right," the man said. He was in his fifties, solidly built, bore the scars on his face and hands of a man who had not always worked behind a counter. "Do I know you?"

"No, but you know a friend of mine," Clint said. "Rick Hartman."

The man smiled.

"I do know Rick," he said. "Haven't seen him in a long time. And who might you be?"

"Also a friend of Rick's," Clint said. "My name is Clint Adams."

"Adams!" Tohill said. "What brings the Gunsmith to my shop?"

"I need help," Clint said. "Rick said you were a man who could be trusted in Yuma. He also said there aren't many."

"There are a few," Tohill said, "but I'm the only one he knows."

"Can we talk?"

"Turn that Open sign to Closed, and I'll break out a bottle of whiskey," Tohill said.

Clint obeyed.

"Come on," Tohill said, "I live in the back."

Clint followed the man into a spacious back room complete with a stove, a table, a chest of drawers, and a bed.

"This is a nice place to live," Clint said.

"It's comfortable," Tohill said. "Sit. I'll get the whiskey."

Clint sat and Tohill brought a bottle and two glasses to the table.

"First, welcome," he said, extending his hand. They shook. "Now drink."

He poured two glasses and handed one to Clint. They both drained them, and Tohill drank another.

"Okay," the gunsmith said, "why don't you tell me what brought you here?"

Clint did, telling the man about his search for Harlan Banks.

"Now it seems he might be in Yuma Prison," he said finally.

"You goin' out there to see?"

"I am."

"And you need backup."

"I've gone this far without it, and I've been lucky," Clint said. "I can't depend on luck anymore."

"Well, you're a friend of Rick's," Tohill said, "and I know your reputation. So just tell me what you want me to do."

"I'm going to ride out to the prison tomorrow," Clint said. "I was thinking of talking to the sheriff today. Would it do any good? Or is he in somebody's pocket?"

"The sheriff is his own man," Tohill said. "He'll talk to you."

"And do you have a police department?"

"We're resisting the Eastern law enforcement agency here," Tohill said, then added, "so far."

"I'm glad to hear that," Clint said. "I'm tired of finding a police chief when I come into a town."

"Like Prescott?"

"Exactly. Okay, so what's the name of the sheriff here?"

"Tucker Coe," Tohill said. "Been the law here for twelve years."

"How old is he?"

"That's just the thing," Tohill said. "He got the job when he was barely thirty, so he's gonna be around for a while."

"As long as he keeps getting elected," Clint pointed out.

"Or until the town fathers do decide to bring in a police department."

"Right."

"When do you want to meet him?"

"As soon as possible," Clint said. "Tonight, even. I do want to ride out to the prison tomorrow."

"Okay," Tohill said. "I'll set it up. Wait at your hotel until you hear from me."

"Will do," Clint said. "And thanks."

"Any friend of Rick's . . ." Tohill said.

Clint went to his hotel, up to his room, and unlocked the door. There was no indication that anything was wrong, no warning. As he walked in, he was hit on the head, and everything went dark.

TWENTY-SEVEN

They came for Clint later at night. He knew the two guards, Ace and Danny.

"Come on," Danny said.

"Where?"

"Somebody wants to see you."

"The warden?"

"You'll see," Danny said. "Come on."

Taking him to see someone, or taking him to be killed? Clint was surprised that no attempts had yet been made on his life. Maybe this was the first one.

Both men were armed. Maybe he could get the gun off one of them. With a gun in his hand . . .

"Come on out," Ace said.

Both guards backed away, leaving plenty of space between them.

"Take it easy, Adams," Danny said. "This ain't nothin' but somebody wantin' to talk to you."

"Yeah," Ace said, "if somebody wants to kill you, we ain't about to help 'em. We ain't gonna get into trouble that way."

Clint didn't know why, but he believed the two of them.

"Okay," he said, coming out of the cell. "Okay."

"Follow me," Danny said.

The slender guard took the lead, and the brute the rear. They marched Clint down several halls, past some cells to the jeers of the occupants, then into another hall with concrete walls but no cells on either side.

At the end of the hall, however, was one single cell. Danny and Ace stopped.

"You go on ahead," Danny said. "We can't let you in, but you can talk. You only got five minutes."

"For what?"

"That ain't for us to know," Danny said. "Just go ahead. We'll wait right here."

"And don't try nothin' funny," Ace warned him.

"What could I try in here?" Clint asked.

Ace didn't have an answer. That was just a warning he used on everybody in Yuma.

"Go," Danny said, "you're wastin' your time."

Clint nodded, and walked toward the cell.

TWENTY-EIGHT

When Clint awoke, he was in the back of a wagon. His gun was gone and his hands were tied behind his back. He looked around, and knew it was a prison transport wagon. He was in it alone.

He was about to call out, but then decided that would be fruitless. Nobody was going to answer him. He had been taken from his hotel, and was now being transported from Yuma to someplace else.

The fact that he was in a prison wagon meant he had been taken by somebody in law enforcement. He had the feeling the man behind this was Chief of Police Henry Blake, or perhaps it was Mayor Halliday's idea. Either way, he figured he was either being taken back to Prescott, or they were taking him to Yuma Prison.

A territorial prison would be the perfect place to stick him, if they didn't want anyone to be able to find him.

He tried the door with his feet, which were tied together, but it wouldn't budge. He settled back against the wall and decided to wait and see where he ended up. If they were going to kill him, they would have done it by now.

Finally, the wagon stopped and he felt it shift as one or two men climbed down from the top. Abruptly, the door was unlocked and opened.

"Come on out, Adams."

He slid toward the door until two pairs of hands grabbed him and yanked him out, dumping him on the ground.

"Cut that out," a voice commanded. "Get him up on his feet."

The two men dragged him to his feet, where he came face to face with Chief of Police Henry Blake.

"What's this about?" Clint asked.

"Murder."

"Murder?"

"You committed murder and fled Prescott," the chief said. "I sent two of my best men to bring you back."

"You're crazy."

"Am I?"

"Who am I supposed to have killed?"

"A woman named Hannah and her son, Ben. They run Hannah's Café."

"What?" Clint said, stunned. "Hannah and Ben are dead?"

"That's it," Blake said. "Act like you don't know anything about it."

"When I left them, they were alive."

"And you left town pretty quickly."

"I had business in Yuma."

"Well, you're back in Prescott now."

Clint looked around and asked, "What part of Prescott is this?"

It was dark and all he saw was the back of a building. He looked around for a few moments, and then suddenly it started to look familiar.

They were behind the Tim Pot Saloon.

"Let's head inside," Blake said. "The judge is waiting."

"The judge?"

"We're going to have a trial."

"Tonight?"

"Right now," Blake said. "Trial, and sentencing."

"So we already know what the outcome of the trial will be," Clint said.

"Well, of course," Blake said. "After all, you're guilty. Everybody knows that."

"And who is everybody?"

"Everybody who matters," Blake said. He looked at his men. "Come on, get him inside."

They grabbed him by his arms and dragged him through the back door, a back room, and into the saloon. He could see that the front doors were closed and barred.

Behind the bar was a man in a black suit, holding a gavel. In the saloon were twelve men sitting in chairs that were lined up against the wall. Clint didn't know any of them, but it was obvious that they were his jury.

"Who's the prosecutor?" Clint asked Blake.

"That would be me."

"And who is acting for my defense?"

"Our esteemed mayor will fill that role," Blake said.

"Oh, great," Clint said. "It's nice that I have someone who believes in me so much."

"Are we ready to proceed?" the judge asked, banging his gavel.

"We're ready, your honor," Blake said.

"The mayor's not even here," Clint said. "If he's my defense, shouldn't he be here?"

"Don't worry," Blake said, "the judge knows what the mayor was going to say."

"This is ridiculous," Clint said.

"This is all legal and aboveboard, I assure you," the chief said.

"That's why we're in a saloon, and not a courthouse?"

"As long as there is a judge," Blake said, "there's a court."

The two guards took Clint to an empty chair and sat him down. His hands were still tied behind him.

"This court is in session!" the judge shouted as his gavel came down on the bar. *Bang!*

Fifteen minutes later the judge said, "Clint Adams, you have been found guilty of murder. I sentence you to life in prison, sentence to be served at the Yuma Territorial Prison outside of Yuma, Arizona. Effective immediately. Court is adjourned." *Bang!*

As the two guards dragged Clint back out the rear door and tossed him into the transport wagon again, he said to Blake, "Why didn't you just have him give me the death penalty?"

They slammed the door closed and Blake put his face to the barred window.

"Anything can happen in Yuma," he said.

TWENTY-NINE

After a week in Yuma, Clint was starting to think he was going to have to break out. But he didn't think he could do that before finding Harlan Banks—alive or dead.

As Clint approached the lone cell, he wondered if he would find Banks inside. Instead, when he reached it, he saw there was a woman inside.

"Clint Adams?"

"That's right."

She was in the shadows, but he could tell it was a woman. For one thing, he could smell her. No perfumes, or lotions, just pure woman. The smell was unmistakable.

She came out of the shadows and he saw she was one

of the women he'd seen in the mess earlier in the week. She was slender and pretty.

"My name is Amanda King."

"What's on your mind, Amanda King?" he asked. "Those two guards said we have five minutes."

"Don't worry about them," she said. "They'll do what I want."

"Why's that?"

"Because I give them what they want."

"Don't they get what they want from all the girls?" he asked.

"Yes," she said, "but I'm the one they don't have to force."

"So when they don't want it to be rape, they pick you?" he said.

"Oh, don't get me wrong," she said. "It's still rape. I've just learned to deal with it on my own terms."

"Well, whatever works for you, I guess," he said. "What's on your mind?"

"I want to get out of here."

"Why tell me?"

"Because you're gonna break out."

"What makes you say that?"

"Because you're the Gunsmith," she said. "You're not gonna let them keep you in Yuma."

"I'm in here for murder," he said.

"So am I. Well, attempted murder anyway."

"I was convicted of two murders—crimes I didn't commit."

"That's where we differ."

"I can't get out of here until I'm proven innocent," he said. "I don't want to break out and be on the run."

"How are you gonna prove yourself innocent if you stay in here?"

"I've got some people on the outside."

"A lawyer?"

"People."

"And they know you're here?"

He hesitated. Ken Tohill would have been looking for him after he disappeared from his hotel. Maybe he and the sheriff would look for him. Maybe Tohill would figure out where he was. Maybe not.

Maybe Amanda King was right. He had to get himself out, and then take steps to prove his innocence.

"Okay," he said, "say I want to get out. Say I do get out."

"Take me with you."

"Why would I do that?"

"You mean aside from the obvious reasons?" she asked, looking him in the eyes.

"I'm not really that anxious to rape you, Amanda," he said.

"With you," she said, "it wouldn't be rape. And I know I don't look so great in here, but you can smell me, can't you?"

"What?"

"I smell like a woman," she said, "and you strike me as the kind of man who likes a real woman."

He stared at her and then said, "You're right about that."

"Also, I can be helpful."

"How?"

"Remember," she said, "I have control of two of the guards. Maybe more."

Clint turned and stole a look at the two guards in question. He was sure she had control of them at times, but more often than not?

"Here they come," she said. "We'll talk again soon. Okay?"

He stared at her hopeful look, and just as the guards reached them, he said, "Sure."

"Okay, that's it," the smaller guard said. "We gotta get 'im back."

"Come on, Adams," Ace said, closing his big hand around Clint's arm.

As they pulled him away from Amanda's cell, he could see how truly frightened the girl really was.

"We'll talk again," he said to her. "Soon."

THIRTY

Back in his cell Clint thought about the things he could have done differently. But there was no point in that, because here he sat, dead sure that, at some point in time, they'd try to kill him. Why else would they have put him in here?

He'd been there a full week and still had not seen the warden. He was starting to wonder if the man even knew he was there. The word had passed through the prisoner population, but did that mean the warden had heard it as well? Not necessarily.

He didn't even know the warden's name. The middle-aged guard with the bulging belly was named Rocco—or "Rock"—and he seemed to have been assigned as Clint's personal guard. In on the frame-up? Maybe not. If he were, he could have killed Clint very easily, anytime.

Rock appeared at the bars and stared in at Clint.

"Don't get used to any special treatment, Adams," he said.

Clint laughed. "What special treatment are we talking about?"

Now Rock laughed roughly. "I know Ace and Danny took you to see one of the girls. I don't know what you did to deserve that."

"That wasn't so special," Clint said. "I wasn't even allowed into her cell."

Now Rock cackled.

"That's about what you deserved."

He walked away, laughing and shaking his head.

Warden Gordon Scott—"Warden Gordon" they all called him—sat back in his chair while the girl undid his trousers and pulled out his flaccid member. Ingrid Simpson was one of the three female prisoners in Yuma at the moment. She was serving six years for stealing some merchandise from a store, then injuring a clerk when he tried to stop her from leaving.

As she worked his penis with her hands, it began to swell. He knew she didn't mind coming to him for this. It was the only time she had sex in the prison that wasn't actually forcible rape. And she didn't care how long it took him to finish. It just meant she was out of her cell longer, and away from the other guards.

Finally, she had him hard enough to take into her mouth. He closed his eyes and let his head fall back as she sucked him. He sat that way, without making a sound, until she sucked his orgasm from him. Then she released his penis, and settled back on her haunches.

He opened his eyes and looked at her. She was a

pretty little thing, about twenty-five. She stared up at him with wide eyes, hoping she had pleased him.

"Very good, Ingrid," he said, and she smiled. "I'll have them take you back to your cell now."

"Must I?" she asked meekly. "Must I go back now, sir?"

"They'd be taking you to the mess for supper, wouldn't they?"

She nodded.

"Don't you like the food?" he asked. "It's better than what the general population gets."

"Yes," she said, "yes, it's fine."

"All right," he said. "You can stay in your cell tonight, and I'll have them bring you something nice."

"But . . . the other girls . . ."

"The other girls didn't suck my peter, did they, Ingrid?" he asked.

"N-No, sir."

"All right, then," he said. "You can go."

"Yes, sir."

She got to her feet. Her slender frame was almost lost inside her clothes. Warden Gordon had never seen her naked. Maybe next time.

He watched as she went out the door, closing it softly behind her. Then he stood up, turned, and stared out his window. Below him was the yard. The prisoners were milling about down there. Occasionally one of them would look up at his window. He knew there were prisoners he never saw in the yard, but he didn't know who they were, or why they were inside. They were not part of the ongoing operations of Yuma Prison. But he also knew there as someone special within the walls, possibly for the past week. He didn't like not knowing who it was.

He knew there were things the prisoners knew that he didn't. He didn't like it, but he didn't have much choice. His masters were playing their games, and while he liked to think of himself as the king of this particular chessboard, the truth was he was little more than a knight. But at least he wasn't a pawn.

He turned away from the window and buttoned up his trousers, then walked to the door and stepped through it.

"Eddie," he said to his deputy.

"Yes, sir."

"See that Ingrid gets a steak brought to her cell. All the trimmings."

"Yes, sir."

"And I'll have two in my office."

"Two?"

"Yes," the warden said. "Two. And have Angus Fowler brought to my office just after the steaks."

"Yes, sir."

He went back into his office.

THIRTY-ONE

Clint sat next to Cates at every meal. The others at the table changed, but it was always Clint and Cates. He had learned to eat the gruel they served the prisoners, but he still gave Cates half of it at each meal. And he ate his bread, minus the moldy bits.

"What's the word, Cates?"

"What word is that, Clint?"

"About when they're going to come for me."

Cates didn't bother to pretend he didn't know what Clint was talking about.

"They're still watchin' you," he said. "They want to see who you become friends with. Who you'll have on your side."

"Why not come for me before that?" Clint asked. "While I'm alone?"

"They're afraid of you."

"Even without my gun?"

"Even without your gun."

"Do you know who'll come for me?"

"No."

Clint looked at him skeptically. "Come on, Cates . . ."

Up to this point Cates had been staring at his food. Now he raised his head and looked at Clint.

"I don't know."

"Can you find out?"

"I might."

"Will you?"

Cates looked at Clint's plate.

"You gonna eat that bread?"

Clint had already picked off the moldy parts, but he hadn't started to eat it yet.

"Be my guest."

Angus Fowler nervously entered the warden's office. He smelled the meat before he entered. The warden was seated at a table, working on a steak with a knife and fork. The plate was filled by the meat, which was accompanied by potatoes, carrots, and onions. Angus's mouth began to water immediately. He saw the other plate across from the warden.

"Hello, Angus."

"Warden."

"Had a bath lately?"

"Two days ago."

"The stench shouldn't be too bad, then," the warden said. "Have a seat, Angus. Eat."

"Eat?"

The warden nodded.

"T-That's for me?"

"Of course," the warden said. "Come on, sit. It's getting cold."

Angus rushed to the table, sat, and picked up the knife and fork. He hastily cut off a hunk of steak and stuffed it into his mouth before the man could change his mind.

"Take your time, Angus," the warden said. "Enjoy the meal. Would you like a glass of wine with it?"

"Uh, yes, sir."

The warden poured Angus a glass of red wine. The prisoner took a gulp, choked for a few seconds, then went back to his meal, this time eating more slowly, but with gusto.

The warden ate his own meal slowly, watching Angus the whole time. Angus was a small man, in his forties, a born victim, usually pretty smelly, usually bruised or battered because one prisoner or another had taken their frustrations out on him. But there was one good thing about him. He'd been in Yuma for fifteen years, and he knew everything that went on in the place. More than any other prisoner, more than the guards . . . and more than the warden.

When the meal was done, Angus sat back and rubbed his belly happily.

"How about a piece of pie, Angus?"

"That'd be great, Warden."

"What kind?"

"Cherry?"

"Okay," Warden Gordon said. "Cherry pie. I'll have it brought in right after . . ."

"After what, Warden?"

"After you answer a couple of questions, Angus."

"Qu-Questions?" Angus suddenly looked worried.

"Just one, actually."

"One question?"

"One won't hurt, will it, Angus?"

"N-No, sir."

"Good," the warden said.

Angus waited, and when the question didn't come, he asked, "W-What's the question?"

"There's a new prisoner," the warden said, "been here about a week. Nobody wants me to know who he is."

"I—"

"But you know, don't you, Angus?"

"Sir, I—"

"I'll have your pie brought in," the warden said, "and coffee. You just answer the question. You know, don't you?"

"Y-Yessir."

"Who is it?"

Angus ducked his head and hunched his shoulders, as if he expected to be hit when he gave the answer.

"Clint Adams."

Surprising himself, Warden Gordon suddenly became incensed.

"The Gunsmith is in my prison?"

"Yessir."

And he didn't know about it? That was unacceptable.

"Exactly when did he get here?" the warden asked.

"You was right about that," Angus said. "A week ago."

"Jesus," the warden said, "they'll kill him in here."

"Yessir."

"Are they plannin' that?"

"Yessir."

"When are they going to try?"

"Geez, I dunno," Angus said. "They's watchin' him to see who's with him."

The warden knew there were other prisoners in his prison that he didn't know about, but this one . . . this one was too big. He should have known about this one!

"Warden, c-can I have my pie?" Angus asked meekly.

"Comin' up, Angus," the warden said. "Your pie is comin' right up."

THIRTY-TWO

Deputy Warden Lloyd Simon watched as the guard walked Angus Fowler out of the warden's office and took him back to his cell.

"Lloyd?" the warden said from his door.

"Yes, sir?"

"Would you come in here, please?"

"Of course."

Simon left his desk, entered Warden Gordon's office, and closed the door.

"What's this I hear about the Gunsmith being in my prison?" the warden asked.

Simon stared at the older man. The deputy warden was in his forties, tall and handsome, and ambitious. He had his eye on the warden's job, and was determined that when he got it, he would know what was going on in every corner of Yuma Prison.

"You're not supposed to know that, sir."

"Well, I do."

"We get paid a lot of money to look the other way on some prisoners."

"But the Gunsmith?" the warden asked. "That's dangerous. Who put him here?"

Simon knew it was the mayor and the police chief of Prescott, but that was also something the warden wasn't supposed to know.

"I hate to think who else is inside these walls I don't know about," the warden said.

"No one else of that ilk, I assure you," Simon said.

"Is he going to be killed here?"

"If he is," Simon replied, "no one will hear about it."

"Jesus . . ." the warden said, rocking back in his chair. "This is too much."

"Relax, Warden," Simon said, "I have everything under control."

"I never should have let you talk me into this."

"Gordon, we're making a lot of money," Simon said. "And having the women here is turning out to be pleasant, isn't it?"

"Well, yes, but—"

"Then continue to be guided by me," Simon said. "I'll handle everything."

Simon studied the warden, hoping that the man was not suddenly acquiring a mind of his own.

In the next moment, his fear was realized.

"I want to see him," the warden said.

"What? See who?"

"Clint Adams," the warden said. "I want you to have him brought to me."

"I don't think that's a very good idea," Simon replied.

"I'm still in command here, Lloyd," the warden said, "despite our little side venture."

"Well, yes, sir, that's true—"

"I want to talk to him," the warden said. "Who do you have on him?"

"Rock is guarding him."

"Excellent," the warden said. "Rock is a good man. Have him bring the Gunsmith to me this evening."

"Sir—"

"Do it, Lloyd," the warden said. "This is not negotiable."

Simon wondered about arguing further, but decided against it. The proper move was probably just to go ahead and get it done.

"All right, Warden," Simons said, "I'll have him brought here this evening. I'm sure he's eating with the others, so as soon as mealtime is over—"

"He's in with the general population?" the warden asked.

"Just for meals."

"I'm not sure that's wise, Lloyd," the warden said. "We'll talk about that after I've seen him."

"Yes, sir," Simon said, "as you wish." He hoped the warden would not notice he was gritting his teeth.

THIRTY-THREE

"You know a man named Harlan Banks?" Clint asked Cates.

Because of everything that had happened in Prescott, this was the first time Clint had asked this question since arriving in Yuma. He didn't want the population to immediately know who he was looking for. He was tired of being lied to every time he mentioned Banks's name.

"Who?" Cates asked.

"Banks," Clint said, "Harlan Banks."

"Naw," Cates said, "don't know 'im."

Clint nodded. They were waiting for the word to return to their cells.

"But that don't mean he ain't here."

"How's that?" Clint asked.

"There are some prisoners inside these walls," Cates said, "who are here . . . let's say, unofficially."

"Is that a fact?"

"Like you," Cates said. "I'll bet there ain't a file on

you in the warden's office. In fact, I'm surprised they bring you in here to eat with us."

"How many prisoners are we talking about?"

Cates shrugged and said, "Maybe half a dozen."

"And what's the point?"

"Money."

"Somebody's paying to have these men held here unofficially?"

"Yup."

"Who's making the money?"

"Deputy Warden Simon," Cates said, "maybe even the warden himself. But Simon's in charge."

"What kind of man is Simon?"

"Easterner," Cates said, "with an education."

"What's his ultimate goal?"

"He wants to be warden," Cates said. "He'll make a lot more money that way."

"Tell me," Clint said, "how long has this been going on?"

"Probably a year and a half. Not long."

"And in that time," Clint said, "have any of those prisoners . . . let's say, disappeared?"

"Oh, yeah," Cates said. "You're askin' me if they been killed? Yeah, the answer's yes."

"But is that the point?" Clint asked. "To bring them in here and have them killed?"

"Don't seem to be."

"Are they ever released?"

"Not that I know of."

"So there are men in here serving unofficial life sentences?"

"I guess you could say that," Cates said. "And your guy may be one of them."

At that point the guards told them to stand and line up. Clint was then yanked from the line by his guard, Rock, and walked back to his cell.

Clint reclined on his cot and thought about what Cates had told him. It seemed obvious that Harlan Banks was one of those "unofficial" prisoners Cates had been talking about. Now what he needed to do was figure out a way to get to him.

And what about the three women? Were they "unofficial"? He hadn't had time to ask Cates about that, but maybe he'd get a chance to ask Amanda—if he got to see her again.

He heard footsteps coming toward his cell, and then Rock was standing just outside the bars.

"Let's go," the guard said. "Somebody wants to see you."

He put the key in the lock and opened the door.

Clint stood up, wondering if he was again being taken to see Amanda. But if so, why by Rock? Why not by her two guards, Ace and Danny?

"Come on, come on," Rock said. "Let's go."

Clint went to the front of the cell and stepped out. Rock then prodded him with his stick.

"Where are we going?" Clint asked.

"You'll see."

They walked down several halls, Rock steering Clint with nudges of his stick. Finally, they came to a door that said WARDEN on it.

"The warden?"

"Quiet!"

If he was being taken to see the warden, did this mean that he wasn't one of the unofficial prisoners Cates had been talking about?

Rock knocked on the door with his stick and said to Clint, "Open it."

Clint did so.

"Inside, Adams," Rock said, placing his stick in the small of Clint's back and pushing him hard. "The man wants to meet you himself."

THIRTY-FOUR

"I'm Deputy Warden Simon," the man at the desk said to him.

"I thought I was being brought to the warden."

"Oh, you will," Simon said. "I just wanted to talk to you first."

"What about?"

"Your treatment while you're a guest here."

"Guest?" Clint asked. "Is that what prisoners here are called?"

"Well, that depends," Simon said, "if you want to be treated like a prisoner, or like a guest."

"What have I been so far?" Clint asked.

"A guest."

"Seems to me I've been a prisoner," Clint said. "Especially given what you've been feeding me."

"You can get better food," Simon said. "You can have a better cell. You can even have . . . company."

"And what do I have to do for all that?"

"Just tell the warden what he wants to hear."

"And what's that?"

"That you haven't been mistreated."

"That's it?"

"That's all."

That wasn't such a stretch. In truth, he hadn't been particularly mistreated to that point—except for the food. And an occasional poke in the back or ribs by Rock's stick. And with the extra benefits, maybe he'd have more of a chance of breaking out. Or finding Harlan Banks.

"Do we have a deal?" Simon asked.

"Why not?" Clint asked.

"Good," Simon said. "I'll take you in now."

He stepped to the warden's door and knocked, then opened it and stuck his head in. "Clint Adams is here," Clint heard him say.

"Good, good," a man's voice said, "bring him on in."

Simon waved at Clint and opened the door wide. Clint walked in.

The portly man behind the desk said to Simon, "That's all, Lloyd. Thank you."

"Yes, sir."

Simon withdrew and closed the door.

"Mr. Adams," the warden said, "I'm Warden Gordon Scott. Please, have a seat."

Warden Gordon, Clint thought, chuckling at the rhyme.

"Can I give you something to drink?" the warden asked. "A glass of red wine?"

"Red wine would be good."

The warden stood up, poured Clint a glass from a

bottle that had already been opened, and handed it to him.

"Thank you," Clint said. He took a sip. Usually, he preferred beer, but after the tepid water he'd been drinking for a week, the wine tasted like nectar.

"I want you to know, it's just come to my attention that you were in my prison."

"Is that a fact?"

"Yes, indeed," the warden said. "I certainly would have had you brought up here long ago if I had known."

"I appreciate that, sir," Clint said. "But now that I'm here, can you tell me why?"

The warden shrugged and said, "Just for a talk. I'd like to make sure you're being treated fairly."

"Well," Clint said, "I'm not even sure what 'fairly' means in a prison."

"Are you being mistreated in any way?" the warden asked.

That was the question Clint was waiting for.

"Mistreated?" Clint asked. "No, I can't say I'm being mistreated. Aside from the fact that I'm in prison for something I didn't do."

"I'm sure you can understand that I hear that quite a bit."

"And I'm sure it's true in a lot of cases."

"Well . . . some," the warden said.

Clint finished his wine. "Is that all you wanted to know?"

"Well . . ."

"Don't you want to know why I'm in here?" Clint asked. "What I was charged with?"

"Yes, of course . . ."

"Murder," Clint said. "I was charged with two murders."

The warden looked surprised.

"I know your reputation, Mr. Adams," he said. "I know you've killed many men, but I never heard anything about you being a murderer."

"That's because I'm not," Clint said. "And if I could get out of here, I could prove it."

"Well, well—"

"I know," Clint said. "You've heard that many times before, too."

"Indeed."

"But in my case it happens to be true. I'm not even sure those murders took place."

"So you were framed?"

"Exactly."

"Why?"

"To get me out of the way."

"Of what?"

"I'm not really sure," Clint said. "Do you know the chief of police of Prescott?"

"No."

"The mayor?"

"No."

No, he wouldn't, Clint thought. Obviously, it was the deputy warden, Simon, who had all the connections.

"Warden, there is something you could help me with."

"What's that?"

"I would very much like not to get killed while I'm in your prison."

"We can probably do something for you on that count," the warden said.

For a moment Clint was going to ask the warden if he'd ever heard of Harlan Banks, but he was sure one of two things was true. Either the warden would say no and mean it, or he'd say no and be lying.

"How about another glass of wine?" Clint asked.

THIRTY-FIVE

Rock took Clint back to his cell, only it wasn't the same cell. This one was in a different part of the prison. It was larger, and the cot had a softer mattress pad on it.

"Better?" Rock asked.

"Some."

"Wait until you have your first meal," Rock said. "This is a whole different part of Yuma."

Now it came to Clint. He thought the route had looked familiar. He was in the same section of the prison that Amanda was in. And maybe the other two girls. And maybe . . .

"Who else is here?" he asked.

"Other guests," Rock said, looking through the bars. "Now just relax, I'm gonna bring you some better clothes. And later you can have a bath."

"Well, well," Clint said, "I'll bet the people in this section of the prison just never want to leave."

"You got that partly right," Rock said.

"Partly?"

"It's not that they don't wanna leave," Rock said. "It's just that they don't."

Amanda took Ace's big cock into her mouth and sucked it, wetting it thoroughly, fondling his balls with one of her hands.

"Aw, geez . . ." he moaned.

"So what do you say, Ace?" she asked. "Do I get to see Clint Adams again?"

"Aw, girl," he said as she slid her tongue along the underside of his cock, "you keep doin' that and you can have anythin' you want."

"What about Danny?" she asked. "Will he go along?"

"Sure," he said, "I can get Danny to do anythin' I want him to."

"Oh, Ace," she said, kissing the head of his cock, "you're my man." She opened her mouth and took him deep inside, then sucked him until he exploded.

Amanda had done much the same thing to Danny a few hours earlier. It had taken her that long to get these two guards when they weren't together.

"Whataya wanna talk to Adams about?" Danny has asked while she sucked his penis. "Unless maybe you wanna do more than talk?"

"Oh, no," she assured him, "you boys keep me plenty busy and satisfied. No, I just want to talk to him. After all, he's a legend."

"Well," Danny said, "legend or not, he ain't gonna last much longer inside."

"All the more reason for me to talk to him," she said, "before he gets killed."

"Oh, all right," he said while she stroked his hard cock, "I can set it up."

"What about Ace?" she asked. "Will he go along with it?"

"Sure," Danny said. "Don't worry about Ace. I'll take care of him."

"You're too good to me," she told him, and took him into her mouth . . .

She'd heard that Clint Adams had been moved, after a meeting with the warden. Now he was in the same section of the prison that she and the others were in. That should make it easier for her to get to see him.

But she knew something was wrong. If the warden knew that Clint Adams was in Yuma, then something was wrong. Usually, he was kept out of the loop when it came to the "special" prisoners. The fact that he wasn't did not sit well with her. If she was going to use the Gunsmith to get herself out of Yuma, it would have to be soon.

Rock found the deputy warden waiting for him just down the hall from Clint Adams's new cell.

"Is he in?"

"Yes, sir."

"Good."

"What's gonna happen now, sir?"

"You'll bring him a nice breakfast in the morning," Simon said, "and then you'll take him for a bath."

"Yes, sir."

"And you'll let him bathe alone. Understand?"

"I understand, sir," Rock said. "He bathes alone."

"And let me know when it's over," Simon said. "Not the warden. Me."

"Yes, sir."

Cates saw the guard come up to his cell and stand with his back to the bars. He got up from his cot and walked to the bars.

"What's goin' on?" he asked.

The guard, Ray Burke, said, "It's gonna be tomorrow."

"Are you sure?"

"That's what I hear."

"How?"

"Rock's gonna take Adams for a bath in the morning, after breakfast."

"They move Adams to the special section?"

"Yeah."

"Ray," Cates said, "I think I feel the need for a bath comin' on."

"It's gonna cost ya, Cates."

"Doesn't it always?"

"Okay, then," Burke said. "After breakfast."

"Okay," Cates said. "Thanks, Ray."

Burke nodded and walked away. Cates went back to his cot. He didn't have any trouble falling asleep that night.

THIRTY-SIX

Clint was surprised to get his breakfast in his cell the next morning. He was also surprised to see what it was.

"Step back," Rock told him.

Clint stepped all the way back to the wall.

"Hands on your head."

He obeyed.

Rock came in, holding his stick in one hand and balancing the tray in another. He set the tray down on the small wooden table—almost a footstool, really. Then he stepped out.

"Okay," Rock said. "Enjoy it."

Clint sat on the cot, pulled the tray over, and took the cloth napkin off. He thought his nose was playing tricks on him, but it wasn't. There it was. Steak and eggs. A couple of biscuits, too. They were hard, but that was okay. They were still better than any of the bread he'd eaten since he first arrived. He had a fork, too, but no knife. Somebody had cut the meat up for him.

The eggs were kind of runny, and the steak well done, but it was the best meal he'd had in what seemed like months. And the topper was the cup of coffee that came with it. It was hot and strong, better by far than the two glasses of wine he'd had in the warden's office.

So far the warden had been true to his word, but the warden wasn't in charge. The deputy warden was. What happened after this meal, and his bath, was anybody's guess.

He decided not to think about it for now, though. He applied himself to enjoying this meal, because he didn't know when he'd have another one like it.

Ray Burke pulled Cates out of the mess after his breakfast, but before they lined up to go back to their cells.

"Ready for your bath?" he asked.

"I don't know," Cates said. "Am I?"

Ray handed Cates something that was easily concealed in their hands.

"Okay, then," Cates said, "I'm ready."

"Let's go," Burke said.

"Finished?" Rock asked Clint.

"Yes."

"Step back, then."

Clint did, put his hands on his head. This time a different guard came in and collected the tray after first making sure the fork was still there. Then he left.

"Ready for your bath?"

"Like you wouldn't believe."

"Let's go, then."

Clint stepped out of the cell and Rock prodded him

ahead. They went down a couple of hallways, didn't pass any other cells, and finally came to a room with bathtubs in it. Both Clint and Rock were surprised to find one of the tubs occupied.

"What the hell?" Rock said.

"What?" Cates asked. "A man can't have a bath?"

"You don't belong here," Rock said.

"Talk to Ray," Cates said. "I ain't gettin' out 'til I'm done."

Rock stood there a moment, unsure of what to do.

"Hey, I don't mind," Clint said.

"Yeah, okay," Rock said. "I'll go get your clean clothes. Don't try leavin' this room."

"Don't worry," Clint said. "Once I'm in the tub, I'm not getting out."

Rock nodded, and left.

Clint walked to a tub that was filled with hot water. Steam drifted up from the surface.

"What are you doing here?" Clint asked.

"Savin' your life," Cates said.

"It's happening today?" Clint asked. "Here?"

"That's what I hear."

"Shit," Clint said, unbuttoning his shirt.

"What are you doin'?" Cates asked.

"I'm taking my bath, damn it," Clint said. "If they're going to kill me, I want to be clean."

"You can't do that!"

"You're in a tub."

Cates stood up, showing that while he had taken off his short, he still had his trousers on.

"Fine," Clint said, tossing his filthy shirt on the floor. "I'll do the same thing." He kicked off his shoes and, with his trousers still on, stepped into the hot water. "Oh, Jesus, this is almost worth dying for."

"Almost?"

"Almost," Clint confirmed.

"Here," Cates said, reaching out his hand.

Clint put his own hand out and Cates dropped something into it. It was a spoon that somebody had spent a lot of time getting a sharp edge on.

"They're liable to come in with real knives," Cates said "You'll need somethin' to defend yourself with."

"Thanks. What about you?"

Cates held up his own spoon and said, "I got one."

"Well," Clint said, "while we're waiting for them to show up, where's the soap?"

"Here ya go," Cates said, reaching out again.

THIRTY-SEVEN

When they came, there were four of them. They entered and spread out, expressionless except for one. He was staring at Cates.

"What are you doin' here?"

"Jesus," Cates said. "A guy can't take a bath in peace?"

"Get out, Cates."

"I'm not done."

The other three didn't seem to care that Cates was there, only the first man.

"If you stay here," the man said, "we're gonna have to kill you, too."

"You mean you'll try," Cates said.

"You asked for it," the man said. "Okay, take 'em."

All four men brandished large knifes, but they thought they were facing two naked, unarmed men. As they approached the tubs, Clint and Cates both stood up and climbed out. Clint noticed that Cates had even kept his shoes on.

They held their makeshift knives ready as the four burly men stalked them.

"Come on," Cates said. "I've been itchin' to kill somebody since I got here."

Since the four men had been instructed to kill Clint Adams, three of them approached him, leaving one man to face Cates.

"Not so big without yer gun, are ya, Gunsmith?" one of them sneered.

"I don't need a gun for a loser like you," Clint said. "Come on."

If the men had a plan of attack, that remark ruined it. The speaker's eyes flared at the insult and he charged, only to take Clint's sharpened spoon right in the gut. Clint pushed him out of the way, and the man fell into the bathtub. His knife sank to the bottom, but Clint didn't have time to reach for it. The other two men were coming at him.

Cates and his man were hand to hand, each having hold of the other's wrist. The other man was bigger and stronger, but Cates turned to his left and stuck out his hip for leverage, took the man over quickly. When he hit the floor, all the air burst from his lungs, and his knife fell from his hand. Cates gutted him with his spoon, then picked up the knife and rushed to Clint's aid.

As the two remaining attackers leaped at Clint, Cates intercepted one of them, darting into the man's path with the knife angled up. The man practically fell on the knife and screamed is it ripped into him.

Clint parried the thrust of the last man, stepped aside as the man lunged past him, then got behind him, slid his arm around his neck, and then cut his throat with the spoon.

He let the body drop to the floor, and it was quiet in the room.

"Get your shirt and shoes and let's get out of here," Cates said. "And take your spoon. This'll look like they killed each other."

"Whoever sent them will know they didn't."

"The two guards, Rock and Burke, will know, too, but they won't say anything," Cates said. "They're not gonna wanna be involved."

They each donned their shirts, and Clint pulled on his shoes.

In the hall Clint said, "Thanks, Cates."

"Keep that spoon," Cates said. "I have a feelin' you're gonna need it again."

They waited outside for each of their guards to return.

"Finished?" Ray Burke asked Cates.

"Oh, yeah," Cates said. "Nice and clean. Wanna check behind my ears?"

Burke ignored him, looked at Clint.

"Who's comin' for you?"

"Rock."

"Well, wait right here for him and don't move."

"Sure thing, boss."

"Let's go," Burke said to Cates.

"See ya later, Clint."

"Cates."

They walked away, leaving Clint alone. He thought

about retrieving one of the knives, but doubted he'd be able to hide it adequately.

When Rock reappeared, he was carrying fresh clothes for Clint.

"I thought I told you to wait inside."

"It's a mess in there," Clint said, taking the dry clothes. "I'd rather change back in my cell."

Rock frowned, looked at the door to the other room. Clint could see the man thinking, should he go in and have a look?

"Okay," Rock said, "come on, I'll take you back."

THIRTY-EIGHT

When word got around about the four men being killed, nobody admitted to knowing anything about it, but according to the story that was circulating, the Gunsmith had killed them himself, with no help. Apparently, he was still deadly, even without a gun in his hand.

Clint sat comfortably in his cell in his new, dry clothes. His second meal of the day was also brought in to him, and then again at supper, he was brought a steak.

"Keeping me away from the general population, boss?" he asked Rock.

"If I had my way, you'd be right in there with them," Rock said.

"Aw, you don't mean that, Rock."

"Shut up and eat your steak," Rock said. "You're gonna have a visitor tonight."

"A visitor? Where?"

"Right here," Rock said, "so finish up and be ready to receive a guest."

                               *   *   *

Clint finished his meal and Rock collected the tray,
making sure he had the fork. He sat back on his bunk
to wait. Eventually, he heard two sets of footsteps coming down the hall. When they appeared in front of his
cell, he saw Rock and Amanda.

"Hello," she said.

"Stay there," Rock said to Clint.

The guard unlocked the door, let Amanda in, and
then closed and locked the door again.

"Call me when you're done," he said to Amanda, who
nodded.

"When you're done?" Clint asked. "Not five
minutes?"

"We've got more time."

"For what?"

She shrugged.

"Whatever you like?"

"Let's talk first."

"Can I sit?"

He slid over on his bunk and she sat next to him. He'd
smelled her when she entered. She smelled like sex. Not
like she'd just had sex, but like sex itself. It wasn't good
for her to be where she was, in a facility with so many
men. Not the way she smelled.

"I want to get out," she said.

"Why tell me?"

"Because of who you are," she said. "You're gonna
get out. All I want is for you to take me with you."

"You want to break out?"

"I don't know how you're gonna get yourself out,"

she said. "Break out, talk your way out, legally . . . I don't know. Whatever."

"You have a lot of faith in me."

"I'm not even sure you didn't get yourself tossed in here on purpose for some reason."

"Uh, no."

"Okay," she said with a shrug.

"What do you have to offer?" he asked. "I mean, that would make me want to help you?"

She stood up and, in one swift moment, dropped her dress. She'd had a bath recently, was clean. Her skin was pale, her nipples pink, her breasts small and firm.

"Amanda, that's not what I meant."

"I could bring you one of the other girls, if you want," she said. "One is older than me, bigger, more experienced, the other very slight, if you like your girls that way. Or you could have two of us at one time."

"Put your dress back on," he said. "I was talking about other, uh, things you might offer."

"Oh." She bent down to grab her dress and pull it back on. "Sorry." She sat back down next to him.

"Don't be. You're . . . very lovely."

"I don't know what else I could offer you," she said. "Except . . ."

"Except what?"

"Well . . . Harlan Banks?"

THIRTY-NINE

"I thought you said you didn't know Harlan Banks," Clint said.

"I don't," she said, "but after you mentioned him, I asked."

"And?"

"He's in here," she said. "I can get you to him."

"How?"

"Leave that to me," she said. "Do you want to see him or not?"

"I do."

"When?"

"As soon as possible," Clint said. "They've already tried to kill me once. I don't expect them to stop."

"I heard about that," she said. "Very impressive."

"Don't believe everything you hear."

"Okay," she said, "I can get you to Harlan Banks tomorrow."

"Why not tonight?"

"I have a favor to ask."

"What?"

"I wanna stay here tonight."

"In my cell?"

She nodded.

"Why?"

"Because if I go back to my own cell," she said, "I'll be raped—again."

"You think they'll let you stay here?"

"I do," she said. "The guards will let me do what I want, as long as I do what they want."

"And what do you do for them?"

"I pretend like it's not rape," she said. "I pretend that I want them to do things to me, or that I want to do things to them."

"Pretend?"

"It's the only way I can get through it," she said. "To let them have what they want."

"And the other girls?"

"They aren't smart enough to do it," she said. "They get raped, forcibly, and they resist. That just makes it worse for themselves, but I can't convince them. They think I'm a slut."

"So they don't get the kind of treatment you get," he said.

"No, they don't."

"That seems to be their problem," he said. "You're doing what you have to do to survive."

"So can I stay?"

"If it's okay with the guards."

"It is."

"Fine, then," he said. "I don't know what the sleeping arrangements will be—"

She stood up, shrugged again, and the dress fell to her ankles.

"You're not gonna make me put it back on again, are you?" she asked.

"Amanda, we just finished talking about rape," he said. "I don't want you to think you have to—"

"But this wouldn't be rape," she said. "This would be because I want to."

"Are you sure?"

"I'm positive."

Clint studied her, felt the heat coming off her naked body, and smelled her—again.

"Please," she said. "I just want to feel wanted, and in control again."

Clint blew out the candle in the cell, pulled the blanket down on the bunk, and said, "Come on, girl."

FORTY

Amanda got into the bunk with Clint, reached into his pants, and took hold of him. He unbuttoned his shirt and took it off, dropping it on the floor. He wondered if the guard would come along and interrupt them.

She crawled down between his legs and peeled off his trousers, then took him in her hand and stroked him. The guards always made her take them in her mouth, but what she wanted to do with Clint Adams was just mount him and then ride him slowly, at her own speed. When the guards stuck it in her, they fucked her hard and fast, until they had their pleasure, and then they left her. She hadn't had any satisfaction since she came to Yuma Prison.

As she mounted him and took him into her steamy depths, she whimpered, almost started crying. Clint let her have her way, riding him for as long as she wanted, and as long as he could hold out before he exploded inside her. They both bit their lips to keep from crying out and then she snuggled up to him beneath the blanket and they went to sleep . . .

In the morning the guard, Rock, woke them and told Amanda, "Come on out."

She got up and, while Rock watched, pulled her dress back on.

"Don't worry," she said, "I'll see you again."

"I'm counting on it," Clint said.

She left the cell, which Rock locked, and they walked away.

Later Rock came with his breakfast and Clint asked him, "What's Amanda in for?"

"She stole a bunch of money," Rock said.

"How much?"

"I hear it was forty thousand dollars," he said, "but nobody knows where she put it."

"Ah," Clint said as Rock walked off. That was why she was getting special treatment. And maybe why he was getting it, too.

Later Rock came to him and asked, "You wanna get some exercise?"

"In the yard?"

"Up to you, the warden said," Rock told him.

Clint didn't see a problem with going into the general population—not after what had happened. It would be a while before they put together another attempt on his life.

"Okay," he said, "let's go."

Rock walked him out to the yard, where he quickly found Cates.

"What the hell are you doin' out here?" Cates asked.

"Relax," Clint said. "I don't think they'll try anything again so soon—and not out in the open."

"Yeah, you're probably right."

"What are you in for, Cates?"

"Banks, stagecoaches, trains," Cates said. "You name it. I was a regular Jesse James."

"You wanna get out?"

"What's on your mind?"

"I'm going to find Harlan Banks today."

"That fella you been lookin' for?" Cates asked. "So he's in here?"

"He is," Clint said, "and when I find him, we're getting out."

"Breakin' out?"

"Unless somebody wants to open the doors for us."

"How?"

"Not sure yet, but I'm going," Clint said. "You want to come?"

"Hell, yeah."

"Okay," Clint said, "be ready for anything, okay?"

"I always am."

Clint stayed in the yard for a couple of hours, mostly just sitting on some stone steps and talking with Cates. At one point one of the guards came walking over to where they were.

"Adams?" the guard asked without looking at him.

"That's right."

"Hang back when they start goin' back inside."

"What for?"

The guard looked at him.

"Hell, do I know?" he asked. "I'm just deliverin' a message."

"Okay," Clint said. "Message delivered, Thanks."

The guard nodded and walked away.

"Could be a trap," Cates said.

"Could be I'm going to see Banks," Clint said.

"You gonna take the chance?"

"That's what life is all about," Clint said. "Taking chances."

"Want me to come with you?"

"No, you've done enough," Clint said. "Like I said, just be ready."

"I'm ready."

Clint nodded. When the guards started taking the prisoners in, he hung back, like he was told. Before long he was alone in the yard.

Alone.

FORTY-ONE

All the doors leading to the interior of the building were closed. Clint remained seated on the stone steps, waiting. Suddenly, one of the doors opened. He was prepared for some more men with knives to appear, but instead one man came out—stumbled out, as if he'd been shoved. He paused, shielded his eyes against the sunlight, then took a few more steps.

The man looked around, still shielding his eyes with one hand. When he spotted Clint sitting on the steps, he dropped his hand and started walking over. Part of the way there he stopped.

"Am I supposed to talk to you?" he asked. "They said I was supposed to talk to someone."

"Harlan," Clint said. "It's me."

The man frowned, shielded his eyes again.

"It's me," Clint said. "Clint Adams."

Banks squinted, said, "Clint?"

"That's right."

"By God, it is you!" Banks said. "You got my telegram."

"I did," Clint said, "but finding you hasn't been easy."

Banks staggered forward, reached out, and grabbed Clint by the shoulders.

"It's great to see you, but . . . are you a prisoner, too?" he asked.

"For the moment."

"But . . . how?"

"Same way as you," Clint said. "Railroaded."

"In Prescott?"

"Yup. Charged with murder. I'm not sure the people I supposedly killed are even dead. At least, I hope not."

"They charged me with killing the telegraph boy."

"Bobby? You're in luck. I spoke to him myself."

"Damn," Banks said, "it's that chief of police, and the mayor. They're as crooked as they come, Clint. I'd planned to expose them through my connections in the state capital."

"And they didn't want you doing that," Clint said, "so they stuck you in here."

"And then you figured out something was going on, and they did the same thing to you. Jesus." Banks sat down. "How the hell are we gonna get out of here now?"

"I'm working on it," Clint said. "We've got some help."

"Who?"

"Well, a prisoner named Cates, and another one named Amanda."

"I don't know them," Banks said. "They been keeping me in solitary."

"I don't understand. If they were so worried about you, why didn't they just kill you?"

"I don't know," Banks said. "Maybe they thought I'd die in here. Or maybe they're planning to kill me soon."

"Have they tried?" Clint asked. "Has anybody tried to kill you?"

"No."

"Well, they tried to kill me," Clint said. "Cates helped me out, but I don't know when they'll try again."

"So what do we do?"

"We get out of here, that's what we do," Clint said. "I'm coming up with a plan."

"Well, you better come up with one fast," Banks said, "before they decide to kill both of us."

"Okay," Clint said. "I'll see if Amanda can get you moved."

"Why would she be able to do that?"

"She has some pull with a couple of guards. And I have the feeling the warden doesn't know anything about you."

"Yeah, that's what I figured, too."

"But he knows about me, because I met him," Clint said, "and maybe it's time for me to talk to him again."

"About what?"

"About me being too famous to die in Yuma Prison on his watch."

FORTY-TWO

Banks was taken back to his cell—wherever that was—and Clint told Rock he wanted to see the warden.

"I ain't supposed to take anybody to see the warden without first checkin' with the deputy warden."

"Well, let's put it this way, Rock," Clint said. "How much would it take?"

Later that day Rock walked Clint down the hall to the warden's office.

"Wait here," he said.

He opened the door and peered in, then withdrew his head.

"Okay, it's like I said. Deputy Warden Simon is out making rounds. Usually takes him a couple of hours. You got that long."

"Okay, Rock," Clint said.

"You won't forget my money?"

"I gave you my word."

"Yeah, you did," Rock said.

Clint went into the office and Rock walked down the hall. At the end of the hall, where there was a bend, he ran into Deputy Warden Simon.

"Is he there?" the man asked.

"Yes, sir."

"All right," Simon said, "it's time to get rid of both of them, Adams and the warden. And I want it to look like escaped prisoners did it."

"Right."

"If you have to kill two or three prisoners to sell that scenario, do it."

"Yes, sir."

"And make sure one of those dead prisoners is Harlan Banks."

"Yes, sir."

"Don't just 'yes, sir' me, Rock. Do it!"

"We will, sir. I've got some good men, like—"

Simon held his hand up.

"I don't want to know," he said. "Just get it done, Rock."

"Yes, sir."

Simon went down the hall and through a door to perform his rounds.

Rock turned, went through another door, where he had six men waiting. They were all guards, but they were dressed as prisoners, and they were armed with guns. Ace and Danny were not among them. They were busy with Amanda again, and did not know what was happening.

"Let's go," Rock told them.

* * *

Clint entered the outer office, where Deputy Warden Simon's desk was empty, made his way to the warden's door, and opened it without knocking.

Warden Gordon looked up from his desk and his eyes widened when he saw Clint.

"Adams!" he said. "How did you get here?"

Clint noticed the warden's hand hovering near a desk drawer. He assumed the man had a gun there.

"Relax, Warden," Clint said. "I just came to talk."

"Where's Simon?"

"He's not out there," Clint said. "I think he's making rounds."

"Well," the warden said, "w-what did you want to talk about?"

"Me," Clint said. "I think we both know I don't belong in here. And we both know there are others inside with the same problem."

"I don't understand—"

"Sure, you do. You've got a special 'unofficial' area of this prison where people disappear. No files, no records, many of them railroad in a kangaroo court, like me, for crimes that didn't happen."

"What do you want—"

"I'm sure you heard four prisoners tried to kill me," Clint said. "They paid for it."

"That was you?" Gordon asked. "You killed all four?"

"That's right."

Again, the warden's hand almost went to the desk drawer, the top one to his right.

"Warden," Clint said, "I think there's something else we can agree on."

"What's that?"

"I'm much too famous to die in here, and have it kept quiet. Don't you think?"

The warden frowned.

"And on your watch," Clint said. "Word would get out quickly, and you'd have some questions to answer. And if the State Prison Board comes in here and takes a closer look at your operation, you'll be in trouble."

The warden bit the inside of his cheek, then said, "It's not me. It's Simon. It was all his idea."

"That doesn't surprise me," Clint said. "Look, there's an easy way for you to avoid this."

"How?"

"Release me," Clint said. "Let me walk out of here with Harlan Banks and Amanda King."

The warden frowned again.

"Who are they?"

"Exactly," Clint said. "You don't know about them, but you're taking the money that's being paid to keep them in here. I think your deputy has taken on a little too much authority here, don't you?"

Actually, the warden did think that. But the extra money, and the sex, had blinded him.

"I need you to get me out of here, Warden," Clint said.

"Yes," the warden said. "Yes."

At that moment they heard something in the other room. Clint lunged for the desk, and the warden thought he was attacking him. But Clint wanted to get to that drawer, and he hoped he was right about the warden keeping a gun in there.

FORTY-THREE

The door slammed open just as Clint got the drawer open and saw the Merwin & Hulbert revolver in the drawer.

As the men came in with guns out, the warden put up his hands and said, "Don't shoot, I'm the warden."

"Yeah," one of the men said, "we know."

Three of the men pointed their guns at the warden, and he knew he was dead. The other three pointed theirs at Clint, but that was a different matter.

Clint grabbed the gun from the drawer, hoping against hope it was fully loaded, because there were six men.

Holding the gun in his hand, he darted over to the warden, who was frozen in place, and shoved him to the floor. At the same time he started firing.

The six men were told they'd be firing at a Gunsmith who had no gun. Seeing the gun in Clint's hand, they panicked. Their shots flew all around Clint as he fired very deliberately.

Two of the guards were blown back into the arms of the others, so their subsequent shots also went wild. These men were prison guards, not gunfighters. They were sent in to perform executions.

Clint fired a third time, and another guard fell. The others were screaming for the falling guards to get out of their way.

A fourth shot dropped a fourth guard. Two left, and Clint hoped he still had two bullets.

The warden was on the floor, curled into a ball with his hands and arms covering his head.

Outside the room Rock heard all the shooting, and rushed inside. On the off chance the warden survived, it had to look like he was rushing to the rescue, routing the escaped prisoners. But when he entered, he was surprised to see four guards down, and the remaining two seemed to be firing with their eyes closed.

Clint pulled the trigger a fifth time, disposing of a fifth guard, and then the burning question was about to be answered.

He pulled the trigger a sixth time, hoping he wouldn't hear the hammer clicking on an empty chamber. The gun fired, and the sixth guard went windmilling out the door into the outer office.

Rock had to step aside to avoid the sixth guard, but then he pointed his shotgun at Clint.

"That's it, Adams," he said, looking around the room. "Six dead guards, six shots. Stand up, Warden."

Warden Gordon stood up and stared at Rock.

"What the hell is going on, Rock?"

"Deputy Warden Simon said it's time to get rid of both of you," Rock said, "and I agree. Who's first?"

"You are, Rock," Clint said, and fired the seventh shot from the rare 7-shot .32-caliber Merwin & Hulbert revolver.

FORTY-FOUR

Clint stood outside Yuma Territorial Prison, dressed in his own clothes, alongside Eclipse, who had been too impressive and valuable an animal for anyone to harm back in Prescott.

When the Yuma doors opened, Warden Gordon came walking out and joined Clint.

"Harlan Banks will be out soon," he said. "Several of the other 'unofficial' prisoners have already been released."

"And the people who put them here?"

"That'll be up to the prisoners, if they want to go back and face them."

"But you'll help?"

"Of course," the warden said. "You saved my life, Adams."

"Well, it was lucky for us that you like rare guns, and you keep one fully loaded. We really needed that seventh shot."

"Yes, indeed."

"What about your deputy, Simon?"

"He's in a cell of his own," the warden said. "I'm, not sure yet, but I might put him in with the general population eventually."

The door opened again and Harlan Banks came walking out, dressed in his own clothes. He took a deep breath of free air, then saw Clint and the warden standing there.

"Mr. Banks," the warden said. "I'm so sorry for what you went through."

"Yeah," Banks said without looking at the warden. "Clint, thanks."

They all shook hands.

"Will you be going back to Prescott for your revenge?" the warden asked.

"Not revenge," Clint said. "Justice. The chief of police and the mayor can't be allowed to keep on the way they are. God forbid one of them actually gets elected to a higher office."

"Sounds to me like they'd be perfect for politics," the warden commented.

"Probably right," Clint said.

"Well," the warden said, "good luck."

"What about Amanda King?" Clint asked.

"Oh," the warden said, "her. Sorry, but I can't let her out. I checked up on her. She actually is guilty."

Clint frowned.

"Sorry," the warden said, and went inside.

As the warden left, Clint said, "Come on, let's get you a horse."

"What about him?" Banks asked. "We just gonna let

him keep running Yuma? Sooner or later he'll miss the money and start up again. Maybe even let Deputy Simon out of his cell to help."

"Nope," Clint said, "we're not going to leave him in there. We'll go to the state capital, and after we've finished exposing Chief Blake, Mayor Halliday, and Deputy Simon, we'll take care of Warden Gordon's career."

Watch for

DEADLY ELECTION

374th novel in the exciting GUNSMITH series
from Jove

Coming in February!

EIGHT

Chief of Police Henry Blake entered the mayor's office, crossed the room, and shook hands with the portly politician.

"Good morning, Henry," Mayor Halliday said. "What can I do for you this morning? Coffee?"

"No, thank you," Blake said. "I've had my breakfast. We have something to discuss, Mr. Mayor."

"Oh? And what would that be?"

The two men sat and eyed each other. Blake had been the mayor's personal choice for chief of police, and believed the younger man was destined to go even further. But he also knew he had to maintain control in their relationship.

"Harlan Banks."

The mayor frowned.

"What about him?"

"There's a man in town looking for him."

"For what purpose?"

"Well, he told one person he was trying to figure out whether a murder charge against Banks was true."

"And?"

"And he told someone else Banks was a friend of his."

"What do you believe?"

"I don't know."

"Well, obviously you think this man is a problem," the mayor said. "Who is it?"

"His name is Clint Adams."

The mayor's eyes widened.

"The Gunsmith?"

"Yes, sir."

"He's in town?"

"He is."

"Well, what the hell . . ."

"My feeling exactly."

"Have you spoken with the man?"

"I have not," the chief said. "He had a talk with the sheriff."

"That old fool?"

"Coyle actually handled himself quite well," the chief said. "Didn't tell Adams anything."

"When do you expect to talk to him?"

"I expect him to come and see me later today."

"Well, you know what you have to do, Chief," the mayor said. "Get rid of him."

"Yes, sir."

"And I mean fast!"

"Yes sir," the chief said. "Fast."

* * *

Clint awoke the next morning with sunlight streaming through the window. From outside he could hear the sounds of wagons passing, people yelling back and forth, the day in a busy town getting started.

He got out of bed, walked to the window, looked out without standing directly in front of it. The main street was bustling. He stepped to the dresser to use the pitcher and basin there to clean up, then dressed, strapped on his gun, and went down to find breakfast.

Actually, breakfast was not hard to find. He decided to go back to Hannah's, where he found the place a lot busier than the day before.

Ben spotted him when he walked in and said, "I saved you a table in the back."

"Thanks."

Clint walked to the back, found the table, and sat. Ben appeared with a pot of coffee and a mug, set them on the table.

"Help yerself," he said, "I'll be back to take your order."

"Steak and eggs," Clint said. "I'll take steak and eggs."

"Okay, comin' up!"

Ben disappeared into the kitchen and Clint poured himself some coffee. He looked around, saw that the town loved Hannah's food as much as he did. There were men, women, and children eating breakfast there. Some of them were looking at him curiously, but most of them were concentrating on their food.

He watched as Ben carried plates out, up and down his arms, and served them without dropping a single one. Finally, he came out carrying Clint's plate and set it down in front of him.

"There ya go!"

"Looks good."

Clint picked up his knife and fork and cut into the steak. Ben watched as he put the first bite into his mouth and nodded his approval, then went back to work.

Clint was halfway through his meal—including a basket of biscuits Ben had brought out—when Sheriff Artie Coyle walked in. He looked around until his eyes fell on Clint, then crossed the room to him, exchanging a few greetings along the way.

"Mornin', Sheriff," Clint said. "Why do I get the feeling you're keeping a close eye on me?"

"Mind if I sit?"

"Pull up a chair," Clint said. "Have some coffee."

Coyle sat and poured himself a cup.

"What's on your mind?" Clint asked.

"A warnin', I guess."

"About what?"

"You're gonna go talk to the chief today, ain't cha?" Coyle asked.

"I am."

"You should know that him and the mayor, they got their own agendas in this town."

"Doesn't everybody?"

"No," Coyle said. "I ain't got one, and I know lots of people who don't. But them two, they're politicians."

"From your tone it sounds like you have the same opinion of politicians that I do."

"I hate 'em!"

"Yeah, we feel the same, all right."

"Well," Coyle said, pushing back his chair, "I just wanted to let you know."

The sheriff stood up, but didn't leave.

"Something else?" Clint asked.

Coyle hesitated. Clint felt the man had something else he wanted to say, but perhaps couldn't figure out how to say it.

"No," he finally said, turned, and left.

Something was on the lawman's mind. Maybe after a few hours to think it over, while Clint talked with the chief, he might find a way to say what he wanted to say.

NINE

In his office, Chief of Police Henry Blake stared out the window at the street below. He stood there, waiting for the Gunsmith to show up. He knew what the mayor wanted him to do, and he intended to do it. He was not intimidated by some Old West legend who was past his prime. These were modern times, and Henry Blake was a modern man. He knew his superior intelligence would serve him well if he came out West, and that eventually he'd be able to work his way back East—to Washington, D.C.

Clint finished eating, paid his bill, and left the café. Ben, busy with other tables, simply waved at him as he went out the door.

From his walks around town the day before, Clint knew where the police station was. He walked that way, taking his time negotiating the busy streets. When he

came within view of the place, he saw a man standing
in a large window on the second floor, looking out.
Instinctively, he knew this was the chief of police.

Clint stood across the street for several minutes, just
watching, making the man wait. Then he realized the
man didn't know what he looked like, so he stepped
from the doorway he was in and walked across the street
to the front door of the police station.

Inside he presented himself to a uniformed policeman standing behind an oversized desk.

"Clint Adams to see the chief, please."

"Do you have an appointment, sir?"

"I think he'll see me," Clint said.

"So he's expectin' you?"

Clint decided to just say, "Yes," and leave it at that.

"Wait here, sir."

The man disappeared into the bowels of the building,
then returned and waved at Clint.

"Come with me, sir."

The policeman led him down a hallway to an open
door, which the man knocked on.

"Chief?" he said. "This here is Clint Adams."

"Thank you, Officer," the chief said. "You can go
back to your desk."

"Yes, sir."

"Come in, Mr. Adams," Chief Blake said. "Have a
seat."

Clint approached the desk and sat down. Neither man
offered his hand. The chief sat also.

"What can I do for you Mr. Adams?"

"I think you know why I'm here, Chief."

"And how would I know that?"

"I'm sure the sheriff has been to see you since yesterday. Told you I came to see him."

Chief Blake smiled. Clint noticed he had very white teeth.

"Let's pretend he didn't come to me," the chief said. "Why don't you tell me what I can do for you?"

"I'm looking for a man named Harlan Banks. I was given to understand that he had passed through Prescott. Do you know anything about him?"

"No, I don't."

"Then I'll have to ride on," Clint said. "To Yuma. Maybe I'll find him there."

"Maybe," the chief said.

"So you've never heard of him?"

"I said no."

"Perhaps the mayor—"

"I doubt it," Blake said. "No one passes through this town without me knowing it."

"So you knew exactly when I arrived?"

"I did."

Clint stood.

"I think I should speak with your mayor."

"Why?"

"I think there might be something you're not telling me."

"Are you calling me a liar?"

"I'm saying maybe you're . . . mistaken."

"And you think the mayor might know something I don't?"

Clint shrugged.

"Who knows?"

"Then be my guest," the chief said. "Go and talk to

the mayor. See what he tells you. But after that, you have to ride out."

"Are you running me out of town?"

"Yes," Chief Blake said. "You've called me a liar. I want you gone, Mr. Adams."

Clint smiled at the chief.

"What's so funny?" the man demanded.

"Driving me out of town," Clint said. "How very Old West of you, Chief."

TEN

Clint left the police department, having learned nothing, but he'd made an enemy of the chief. The man wanted him out of town by tomorrow, but if Clint didn't find Harlan Banks by then—or, at least, word of him—it would be time for him to leave anyway. His next stop would be Yuma, but first . . . the mayor.

He went to City Hall, presented himself to the mayor's secretary.

"You don't have an appointment," the severe, middle-aged woman said.

"No, I don't," Clint said, "but I think he'll see me. The chief of police sent me."

"Chief Blake?"

"That's right."

"One moment, please."

She stood up and went through a door behind her,

presumably into the mayor's office. When she came
back, she said to Clint, "He'll see you."

Clint had gone this route many times before, been in
the offices of many mayors in many towns. Certain ritu-
als were repeated from town to town. There was no way
around it. Leaving his horse at a livery, registering at a
hotel, that first beer and first steak after the trail.

The mayors he had met in the past usually fell into
two categories. All were politicians, but some were satisfied with their job, while others wished to use it as a
stepping-stone to bigger things. Having already met the
chief—and talked to the sheriff—he had a feeling he
knew what kind of man Mayor Halliday was.

He entered the office. The mayor was a large man,
broad in the shoulders, had not gone soft like many
politicians did behind a desk.

The man didn't look happy.

"I understand you just came from the chief of police."

"I have."

"Why would he send you here?"

"He didn't send me," Clint said. "I told him I was
coming."

"You told my secretary—"

"I lied," Clint said. "It was a little white lie, though."

"I don't like jokes, Mr. Adams."

"This is no joke, Mayor," Clint said. "I'm here looking for a man named Harlan Banks. Everyone I've
talked to—bartenders, storekeepers, the law—all claim
to have never heard of him."

"What's that got to do with me?"

"I'm giving you a chance to be the only one to tell
me the truth."

"The truth being?"

"That Harlan Banks was here," Clint said. "And while you're at it, you can tell me where he went. Or what happened to him."

"I could do that, except . . ."

"Except?"

"Except that I've never heard of Harlan Banks," the mayor said.

"Which is what everybody else in town says."

"Maybe that's because it's the truth," the mayor said. "Maybe this Banks fellow is in Yuma."

Clint stared at the mayor. Was he telling him that Banks was in Yuma?

"Why don't you go there?"

"And get out of Prescott?" Clint asked. "Funny, that's what the chief told me."

"Then he's doing his job."

"So," Clint said, "let me get this straight, Mr. Mayor. Nobody in this town has ever heard of Harlan Banks?"

"That's correct."

"Okay," Clint said. "Well, then, I guess I'm done here."

"So you'll be leaving?"

Clint stood and nodded.

"In the morning, yes."

"I hope you enjoyed your stay in Prescott, Mr. Adams," the mayor said.

"Well, no, I didn't," Clint said.

The mayor did not respond to that.

"Thank you for seeing me, Mr. Mayor."

Clint turned and headed for the door.

"Would you do me a favor?" the mayor asked.

"Sure, why not?"

"Send my secretary in on your way out."

"Sure thing."

He stopped at the woman's desk and said, "He wants to see you now."

"Right now?" she asked.

"Yes," Clint answered, "that's what he said, right now."

She remained seated behind her desk, staring at him. He realized she wasn't going to move until he was gone. He entertained the thought of just standing there and seeing if he could outlast her, but in the end he turned and left.

ELEVEN

As the secretary entered his office, the mayor stared out the window with his hands clasped behind his back.

"You wanted me, sir?"

"Yes," he replied without turning. "I need you to send a message to the chief of police."

"Of course, sir."

"I want him here as soon as possible."

"But . . . he was just here this morning, wasn't he?" she asked.

He turned and looked at her over his shoulder,.

"Don't be addled, Margaret," he said. "Of course he was here. You saw him."

"Yes, sir, I did."

"I want him here again," he said, "and as soon as possible. Get that message to him."

"Yes, sir," she said. "Of course."

She turned and left the office. The mayor turned his attention back to the window.

*　*　*

Clint left City Hall and went directly to the telegraph office.

"Can I help ya?" the clerk asked. He was a man in his fifties, very pale from hours spent inside, very thin except for a bulging belly.

"I received a telegram sent from this location," Clint said. "I'd like to know if you sent it."

"Um, well, I guess . . . can I see it?"

"No."

"But then, how can I tell—"

"It was a few weeks ago," Clint said. "The man would have been in his thirties, with blue eyes and a scar here." Clint touched the spot next to his left eye.

"I don't . . . that doesn't sound familiar, sir," the man said nervously.

Was everyone in this town a liar? Clint wondered.

"Does anyone else work here?"

"No, sir," the man said. "Only me."

"I see." He could have asked if anyone had been working at the telegraph office several weeks ago, but the man would only have lied again.

"Okay, thank you."

Clint left the telegraph office, paused just outside. Who was the only person in town who had not lied to him—yet?

Clint walked to Hannah's Café. There was only one man seated at a table, eating. Ben was nowhere to be seen, but at that moment he came out from the kitchen.

"Hey, can't keep you away from here," he said.

"I'm not here to eat," Clint said. "I need to ask you a question."

"Okay, ask."

"Can we sit?"

"Sure. Want some coffee? No charge."

"Okay."

Clint sat at the same back table he'd occupied at breakfast while Ben went into the kitchen. He returned with coffee and a piece of pie.

"Peach," he told Clint. "Also no charge."

Clint put a hunk into his mouth. It was sweet as sugar, the peaches soft but not mushy.

"It's great," he said, washing it down with coffee.

"What was the question?"

Clint looked around. The lone man was paying attention to his food, and nothing else.

"So far everyone I've talked to in this town has lied to me, except you," he said to the young man.

"Lied about what?"

"Harlan Banks."

"Really, Clint," Ben said, "I never met the man."

"That's okay," Clint said. "I believe you. My question is about something else entirely."

"What's that?"

"The telegraph office," Clint said. "Do you know how many key operators there are?"

"One," Ben said. "His name's Lenny."

"Pale as a ghost?"

"That's him."

"No one else?"

"Nope," Ben said. "Just him."

Clint frowned, had another slice of pie.

"What about a few weeks ago?"

"Oh, well," Ben said, "back then there was two."

"There was?"

"Sure," Ben said, "my friend Bobby worked there."

"And what happened to Bobby?"

"He got fired."

"What for?"

"He never told me."

"Did you ask?"

"I did," Ben said. "A couple of times. He said he couldn't tell me."

"I'd like to meet your friend Bobby," Clint said. "Can you arrange that?"

"Sure," Ben said with a shrug, "why not?"

"Good. Today?"

"Now, if you want," Ben said. "I'll take you to his house."

"That's fine," Clint said. "Thanks."

Ben stood up.

"You finish your pie. I'll take care of my last customer and tell Mom."

"Okay."

Ben went into the kitchen. Clint looked over at the man, who was dressed poorly, eating with dirty hands. The man looked at him and smiled.

"The food here is real good," the man said.

"Very good," Clint said.

The man nodded, smiled, and ate his last bite.

TWELVE

As they walked away from the café, Clint asked, "Tell me about the man who was eating."

"That's Randy. He's broke, so we feed him when we can."

"The town drunk?"

"Oh, no," Ben said, "he's just fallen on bad times, is all. He does odd jobs around town, but he hasn't had one in a while."

"Why not give him a job?"

Ben laughed.

"Mom won't have him around the café for any longer than it takes him to eat," he said. "And only if there are no other customers."

"I see. Tell me about your friend Bobby."

"Well, he had the job as a key operator for a few months, then suddenly got fired. He won't tell me why. Now he does odd jobs."

"Like Randy?"

"Not quite like Randy," Ben said. "Bobby has a house, he pays his bills, he's a hard worker."

"Then what happened with the key operator job?"

Ben shrugged and said, "Maybe he'll tell you."

The house was a small shack just outside town. Ben led Clint to the front door, which he knocked on loudly.

"He might be out back workin'," Ben said, but at that moment the door opened and a slender young man, Ben's age or a little older, appeared.

"Yeah? Hey, Ben. What brings ya out here?"

"I got a friend here wants to ask you some questions, Bobby," Ben said. "This is Clint Adams."

Bobby looked at Clint for a moment before recognition dawned in his eyes.

"The Gunsmith?"

"That's right."

Bobby looked at Ben. "He's a friend of yours?"

"Sure is. You mind if we come in?"

"Huh? Oh, uh, no, come on in."

They entered, closing the door behind them. It was one room with a cot, a table, a potbellied stove. There was a pot on top of it with something crusted inside.

"I, uh, ain't got nothin' to drink," Bobby said.

"That's okay," Clint said. "We won't be here long."

"So . . . what's the Gunsmith doin' in Prescott?" the young man asked. "And whataya want with me?"

"It's very simple," Clint said. "A few weeks ago I got a telegram from this town. It was sent by a friend of mine. I believe you sent it to me. And then you got fired."

Bobby looked down, stuck his hands in his back pockets.

"I—I ain't supposed ta talk about that."

"I understand," Clint said, "and I'm not going to tell anyone. Neither is Ben."

"Well . . . okay."

"My friend's name in Harlan Banks. That name mean anything to you?"

"Banks?" Bobby thought, furrowing his brow. "I don't remember that name."

"Maybe you'll remember this," Clint said, taking the telegram from his pocket. "Go ahead, read it. See if it jogs your memory."

Bobby took the telegram, read it quickly, then handed it back. He immediately stuck his hands beneath his arms.

"I don't remember."

"I think you do, Bobby," Clint said. "Why'd you get fired?"

The boy shrugged and said, "They said they didn't need me no more."

"Who told you that?"

"Lenny."

"It was the other operator who fired you?"

"Yeah."

"And he didn't tell you why?"

"H-He didn't really know," Bobby said. "He said he was sorry, but he was told ta fire me."

"Told by who?"

"The mayor."

"The mayor himself?"

"I dunno," Bobby said. "Maybe he sent a message, but it came from the mayor."

"Okay, Bobby," Clint said. "You know why you were fired. Tell me."

Bobby bit his lip.

Clint took out some money and showed it to the boy. It was more than he'd earn from odd jobs in a week.

"Come on," Clint said, "answer the question, and then you can go and get a good meal."

"Go on, Bobby," Ben said. "Nobody's gonna know."

Grudgingly, Bobby reached out and accepted the money.

"I got fired for sendin' that telegram," he said.

"And my friend sent it himself?" Clint asked. "Tall man, blue eyes, with a scar here?"

"That was him."

"Was he in trouble?"

"I dunno."

"What did he say?"

"Just that he wanted to send that telegram."

"Then what?"

"He left."

"Did you ever see him again?'

"No."

"When did you get fired?"

"'Bout an hour later."

Clint handed Bobby the money.

"Has anybody talked to you since then?"

"When Lenny fired me, he said he was sorry, but I shoulda asked somebody before I sent that telegram." He screwed up his face and whined, "How was I to know?"

"You couldn't."

"I really liked that job."

Clint felt sorry for the boy, took out some more money, and handed it to him.

"Get yourself cleaned up, buy some food," Clint said. "You'll get another job."

"Maybe I don't want another job in this town."

"Can't say I blame you," Clint replied.

THIRTEEN

Clint and Ben left the house and headed back to town.

"So you figure your friend was in a jam?" Ben asked.

"That's the way it looked."

"He didn't say that in his telegram?"

"He said he was charged with murder in Prescott, and he asked me to come running," Clint said.

"That sounds like a heap of trouble."

"Yeah. So I came to find him," Clint said. "But where did he go from the telegraph office?"

"Coulda been anywhere," Ben said, "but I know he never came to eat at our place."

"And why not?" Clint asked. "Best food in town, right?"

"Maybe he didn't have a chance," Ben said.

"And if that's the case, why not?"

They reached town and started walking down the main street, which in Prescott was First Street.

"You got any idea when he got here?" Ben asked.

"No," Clint said, "so I don't know how long he was here before he sent me the telegram."

"He didn't register in a hotel?"

"I haven't checked them all," Clint said, "but I have a feeling I'll find that he didn't—even if a few pages got torn out of a register book."

"If you want, I could ask around," Ben said. "I know most of the clerks in town."

"I don't want to get you in trouble," Clint said, "or put you in danger."

"I won't be in no danger," Ben said. "I'll just be askin' some friends some questions."

"What about your mother?" Clint said. "I don't want to get into trouble with her."

"Don't worry," Ben said. "I'll be able to ask questions and still do my work."

"Okay," Clint said, "but be careful who you ask and who hears you ask your questions."

"Don't worry, I will," Ben said.

They reached Clint's hotel, where they split up. Clint went into his hotel while Ben continued on to the café.

In the lobby the desk clerk noticed him and called out, "Mr. Adams?"

Clint walked over to the desk.

"Sir, I have a message for you."

"From who?"

"I wouldn't know that, sir," the man said. "I found it waiting for me here on the desk. I put it in the slot for your room."

"Okay," Clint said. When the man didn't move, Clint added, "I'll take it now."

"Yes, sir."

The man turned, retrieved an envelope, and passed it to Clint.

"Thank you."

Clint decided to take it to his room to read it. When he got inside, he opened the envelope and took out the slip of paper. The handwriting was neat and legible, the kind of thing you'd expect to see from a woman.

I have some information for you. Meet me at ten o'clock at the Tin Pot Saloon.

Clint had seen a saloon with that name while he'd been in town. But would a woman pick a saloon as a meeting pace? It seemed fairly obvious that this was some kind of trap. But what was he being set up for? A beating? A frame-up? Or to be killed himself?

If Harlan Banks had been killed, then there'd be no hesitation to kill his friend as well. But if someone was trying to cover up a murder, wouldn't they have gotten rid of Bobby, the key operator, instead of just firing him?

It seemed Clint had no choice but to keep the appointment, stay alert, and see what happened.

THE GUNSMITH

373

TICKET TO YUMA

J. R. ROBERTS

JOVE BOOKS, NEW YORK

THE BERKLEY PUBLISHING GROUP
Published by the Penguin Group
Penguin Group (USA) Inc.
375 Hudson Street, New York, New York 10014, USA

Penguin Group (Canada), 90 Eglinton Avenue East, Suite 700, Toronto, Ontario M4P 2Y3, Canada
(a division of Pearson Penguin Canada Inc.) • Penguin Books Ltd., 80 Strand, London WC2R 0RL,
England • Penguin Group Ireland, 25 St. Stephen's Green, Dublin 2, Ireland (a division of Penguin
Books Ltd.) • Penguin Group (Australia), 250 Camberwell Road, Camberwell, Victoria 3124, Australia
(a division of Pearson Australia Group Pty. Ltd.) • Penguin Books India Pvt. Ltd., 11 Community
Centre, Panchsheel Park, New Delhi—110 017, India • Penguin Group (NZ), 67 Apollo Drive,
Rosedale, Auckland 0632, New Zealand (a division of Pearson New Zealand Ltd.) • Penguin Books
(South Africa) (Pty.) Ltd., 24 Sturdee Avenue, Rosebank, Johannesburg 2196, South Africa

Penguin Books Ltd., Registered Offices: 80 Strand, London WC2R 0RL, England

This is a work of fiction. Names, characters, places, and incidents either are the product of the
author's imagination or are used fictitiously, and any resemblance to actual persons, living or dead,
business establishments, events, or locales is entirely coincidental.

TICKET TO YUMA

A Jove Book / published by arrangement with the author

PUBLISHING HISTORY
Jove edition / January 2013

ISBN: 978-0-515-15129-9

JOVE®
Jove Books are published by The Berkley Publishing Group,
a division of Penguin Group (USA) Inc.,
375 Hudson Street, New York, New York 10014.
JOVE® is a registered trademark of Penguin Group (USA) Inc.
The "J" design is a trademark of Penguin Group (USA) Inc.

PRINTED IN THE UNITED STATES OF AMERICA

10 9 8 7 6 5 4 3 2 1

ALWAYS LEARNING   **PEARSON**

ONE

YUMA TERRITORIAL PRISON

The iron door closed with a loud clank. The key turned
with a lower click. Clint Adams had been in a lot of
small rooms in his time, but never anything as small as
this cell. He looked around. There was a cot with a worn
blanket and a hole in the ground to use as a privy. He
sat on the cot, found it as hard as sitting on the ground.
Leaning against the wall, he thought back to how he
had become an inmate in Arizona's famed Yuma
Prison . . .

A FEW WEEKS EARLIER

Clint rode into Prescott, Arizona, looking for a man
named Harlan Banks. Prescott had undergone a growth
spurt over the past few years, and was now a thriving
community with more than several saloons and hotels.

The streets were busy as he rode in at midday, and he had to rein in several times to avoid colliding with a wagon, a pedestrian, or another horse.

Prescott was too big to be able to find one man easily, unless you knew where to look. For a man like Banks, you looked in saloons—but not just any saloon. The ones that featured not only whiskey, but also gambling and girls. However, first you looked in jail, because a man like Harlan Banks invariably found himself behind bars at one time to another.

Clint rode through town, filing away locations in his brain. Gambling parlors, hotels, cafés, the sheriff's office, and a police station. He kept going until he came to a livery stable. He dismounted and walked Eclipse inside.

"Whoa," the man inside said, "that's some animal."

"Yeah, he is," Clint said.

The man was in his sixties, had the scars to prove he'd been around horses most of his life. At some time or other a horse had nipped his face, his hands, he was even missing half of a finger that some horse thought was a carrot. And he limped, indicating he'd probably been kicked more than once.

He knew good horseflesh when he saw it.

He walked around Eclipse, ran his hand over the horse's withers. Clint was surprised that the Darley Arabian allowed it. There must have been something about the man that the horse liked.

"What's your name?" Clint asked.

"Folks call me Handy."

"Well, Handy, I want him well taken care of," Clint said. "Does that mean I leave him with you?"

"It sure does," Handy said. "I'll take care of him better than anybody in town could."

"Okay," Clint said. He removed his rifle and saddlebags, allowed Handy to take Eclipse's reins.

"He got a name?" Handy asked.

"Eclipse."

"Nice name," Handy said. "You got a name?"

"Clint."

"Where you gonna be, Clint?"

"A hotel," Clint said.

"Which one?"

"Don't know," Clint said. "I just rode in. You got a suggestion?"

"Statler House, down the street," Handy said. "Not the best in town, but clean, with good mattresses."

"That sounds like the best hotel in most towns."

"Well, this town's growin'," Handy said. "Coupla other hotels got what they call honeymoon suites. Ya pay lots for that kinda room. That what you're lookin' for?"

"Nope," Clint said. "No honeymoon for me. Clean is good enough."

"There ya go," Handy said.

"How much, Handy?"

"I dunno," Handy said. "Why don't we talk about that later? Ask anybody. I won't gouge ya. In fact, maybe I'll end up payin' you."

"Okay, Handy," Clint said. "We'll talk about it later."

"There ya go," Handy said again.

Clint turned to leave, then turned back.

"I've got a question."

"Yeah?"

"I need to talk to the law," Clint said. "I'm lookin'

for a friend of mine, usually gets himself in trouble in saloons. Do I need to talk to the sheriff, or go to the police station?"

"Police station," Handy said, as if the words tasted bad. "They call that progress. Naw, if you're friend needed a night in jail, he woulda gone to the jail. You wanna talk to the sheriff."

"What's he like?"

"His name's Artie Coyle," Handy said. "Been sheriff here over a dozen years."

"That's a long time."

"Folks like him," Handy said. "But then the town council, they decide we need a police department, like back East."

"It's happening a lot in the West," Clint said.

"So now Artie, he handles drunks and stray dogs. Most everythin' else goes through the new police department, and their chief of police."

"What's he like?"

"Like a store clerk somebody pinned a badge on," Handy said.

"How many men on the police force?"

"Maybe a dozen."

"They wear uniforms?"

"Oh yeah, carry guns and sticks. Some of them, they use them sticks a little too much."

Clint nodded.

"Okay," he said, "thanks, Handy. I'll be at the Statler, as long as they have a room."

"They got a room," Handy said. "Just tell 'em I sent ya."

"Thanks, Handy."

TWO

Clint checked into the Statler, found that Handy was right. Mentioning his name got him a room with no questions, and it was clean. He sat on the mattress for a moment, found it very comfortable.

He walked to the window to check on his view, and access. Satisfied that he could see most of the street, and access to his window would be difficult, he left his rifle and saddlebags and went back to the street.

He walked for a while before coming to the sheriff's office. It was easily one of the oldest buildings in the town. He'd been finding this true of many Western towns that were growing. He didn't much care for the towns where East was meeting West in the name of progress, but there was nothing he could do about it.

He entered the office, found a man in his sixties sitting behind the desk with a badge on his chest. He was looking at wanted posters the way most people looked at keepsakes from their past.

"Excuse me?"

The sheriff looked up from his desk, gave Clint a sad look.

"Yeah?"

"My name's Clint Adams," he said, figuring he might as well start there.

The sheriff's face brightened.

"The Gunsmith?"

"That's right."

"Well . . . have a seat, Mr. Adams," the lawman said. "It's a pleasure to have you here. My name's Sheriff Artie Coyle."

Clint came forward and took a seat across from the man, who suddenly seemed very happy. It must have seemed to him that a shadow of the Old West had entered his office.

"What can I do for you?" Coyle asked.

"I'm looking for a man," Clint said. "My information is that he came through here."

"Oh? Who'd that be?"

"His name's Harlan Banks."

"I know that name," Coyle said.

"From where?"

"I don't know." The lawman's gaze fell upon his collection of posters. "Maybe there's paper on him."

"I don't think so," Clint said. "Not yet anyway."

"Well, what'd he do?"

"He's supposed to have killed someone," Clint said.

"You don't know for sure?"

"No," Clint said, "that's why I want to find him. To ask him."

"So you ain't gonna kill 'im on sight?"

"No," Clint said, "I have to talk to him first."

"And then kill 'im?"

"If he did kill someone," Clint said, "I'll bring him in myself to face trial and watch him swing."

Coyle screwed up his face in concentration.

"It'll come to me," he said finally. "You stayin' in town?"

"I'm at the Statler."

"Good," Coyle said. "I'll know where to find you when it comes to me."

"Do you think he might have passed through town?" Clint asked.

"Could be."

"Maybe I'll talk to some of the bartenders in town," Clint said. "One of them might have something to tell me."

"There ya go," Coyle said.

Clint got up, started for the door, then turned and asked, "You got a brother in town?"

"No," Coyle said, "but I got a cousin."

"Runs the livery. Named Handy?"

"That's right. How'd you know that?"

"Lucky guess," Clint said. "I'll be seeing you, Sheriff."

"If you're lookin' for a good meal," Coyle said. "try Hannah's Café, on Second Street. Great steaks."

"Sounds good," Clint said. "Thanks."

Outside Clint thought about checking the saloons, but his stomach growled. That convinced him to go and find Hannah's right away instead.

He walked to First Street, then Second, and found

the café. As he entered, he saw that only a few tables were taken, as it was after lunch but before supper.

"Help ya?" a young waiter asked. He was tall and thin, maybe twenty, with a clean white apron on, like he'd just donned it.

"Just rode into town and I've got a powerful appetite. The sheriff told me to come here."

"You a friend of the sheriff's?" the boy asked.

"We just met," Clint said. "But he told me this place has the best steak in town."

"Take a table," the boy said. "I'll tell Ma to make ya one."

"Your Ma Hannah?" Clint asked.

"Yeah, how'd you know?"

"Um, that's the name of the place, right?"

"Oh, yeah, sure," the kid said. "You want some coffee?"

"Yeah, a pot," Clint said. "Thanks."

He sat at a table while the boy disappeared through a door, presumably to the kitchen.

There was a middle-aged couple sitting across the room from him. They both nodded and smiled, so he returned the greeting.

The boy came out with a pot and a mug and set them down on the table.

"Steak'll be out in a coupla minutes, mister," he said.

"Thanks."

Clint poured himself a mug of coffee. From the smell he knew it would be strong, the way he liked it. It was also hot. It made him hopeful for the steak.

THREE

"How was it?" the young waiter asked when he collected the empty plate.

"Can't you tell?" Clint asked.

"Yeah, the plate looks almost like you licked it," the kid said. "Dessert?"

"Is your mom's dessert as good as her steak?"

"Oh, yeah."

"What do you have?"

"Pie."

"Peach?"

"Not today," he said, "but she does have apple, rhubarb, and blueberry."

"Blueberry?" It had been a long time since Clint had blueberry pie. "I'll have that one."

"Comin' up."

"And more coffee."

By the time the kid brought the pie out, the place was

empty, except for Clint. So when he came out with the pie, his mother came behind him with the coffee.

"This is my mother, Hannah," the kid said.

"You're his mother?" Clint asked, looking at the beautiful young woman as she poured him some more coffee.

"I am," she said. She stood up and put her hand on her son's shoulder. "He's a fine boy. Enjoy your pie."

She turned and went back to the kitchen.

"How old—how old are you?" Clint asked.

"Me?" the boy said. "I'm nineteen. Mom was sixteen when I was born."

The boy returned to the kitchen. Clint attacked the pie, found it every bit as good as the rest of the meal. He wondered if she'd be able to combine the blueberry pie with peach, if he asked her to.

The next time the boy came out, Clint asked, "What's your name?"

"Ben."

"That was a great meal, Ben," Clint said. "Be sure to tell your mom I enjoyed it."

"Well, if you're stayin' in town, come by again," the kid said. "You can try her beef stew."

"I'll do that," Clint said. "Thanks."

As Clint headed for the door, Ben said, "I think there's peach pie tomorrow."

"I'll remember," Clint promised.

FOUR

Later Clint stopped into a saloon called The Red Garter. It was doing a good business for that time of day, considering the gaming tables were still covered and there was only one girl working the floor.

Clint went to the bar and ordered a beer from a bored-looking bartender. He wondered how soon he'd be hearing from the sheriff, or maybe even the chief of police.

Sheriff Coyle watched from his window as Clint entered The Red Garter Saloon. Satisfied that Clint wasn't on the street, he grabbed his hat, strapped on his gun, and left the office.

He walked a few blocks away to the new police department building and entered.

"Afternoon, Sheriff," the uniformed policeman on the front desk said. "What can I do for you?"

"Please tell the chief I'm here to see him."

"I think he's busy—"

"Tell him it's about Harlan Banks," Coyle said. "I think he'll see me."

"Wait just a minute."

The desk man disappeared down a hallway, then reappeared moments later and said, "You know where his office is, don't you?"

"Oh, yeah," Coyle said.

He walked down the hall to the man's office and knocked on the open door.

"Arthur," Chief of Police Henry Blake said. "Come on in."

Coyle entered, looked at the chief's proffered hand a moment before shaking it. Henry Blake had actually not been a store clerk before he became the chief of police in Prescott, Arizona. He'd been the headmaster of a school back East. But he came to Prescott with an impressive education and the town council hurriedly hired him before he could change his mind.

"Have a seat, Arthur."

Even though the chief was about fifteen years younger than the sheriff, Coyle always felt like a boy in the headmaster's office when he came to see him. On the other hand, Chief Blake never came to see the sheriff in his office.

"What's on your mind, Sheriff?"

Whenever anyone in uniform—or the chief, who wore expensive three-piece suits—said "Sheriff," it was always with a smirk in their tone.

"I had a visitor today," the old-time lawman said.

"Yes? A stranger to our fair city?"

City. To Coyle, Prescott was still a town, but the chief of police always referred to it as a city.

"Yes, a stranger to Prescott," Coyle said, "but not really an unknown."

"This sounds very mysterious," Blake said. "Who was it?"

"Clint Adams."

Blake stared at the sheriff for several seconds without comment.

"The Gunsmith," Coyle said.

"Yes, yes, I know who Clint Adams is, Sheriff," Blake said. "I was waiting to hear why I should be concerned with this development."

"Because," Sheriff Coyle explained, "he said he's here lookin' for Harlan Banks."

That made the chief frown, giving Coyle some small feeling of satisfaction.

"Did he say why?"

"Claims he heard that Banks killed someone," Coyle said. "Says he wants to find out if it's true."

"Not kill him?"

"No."

"Isn't that odd for a gunman like him?" the chief asked.

"You can't always believe what you hear, Chief," Coyle said. "Especially what you hear back East. Wild West stories just seem to grow between here and there."

"So he's not a gunman and a killer?"

"He has a reputation for being good with a gun," Coyle said. "Possibly the best ever. He does not have a reputation for being a killer."

"But he has killed people, right?" Baker asked.

"Uh, well, sure, I suppose so," Coyle said.

"All right, then," Baker said. "In my book, that makes him a killer. And in my city, it's my book that counts."

"So what do you intend to do?" Coyle asked.

"I'll meet with the mayor and the town council," Baker said. "Among us we can come up with a course of action. Meanwhile, how long is he staying?"

"He didn't say," Coyle answered.

"Well," the chief said, "maybe you should find out."

"Me?" Coyle asked. "I'm not part of your department. Why wouldn't you have your own man do it? Or do it yourself?"

"Because you and Adams have something in common," Blake said. "You are both remnants of a bygone time."

"You think he'll talk to me, but not to you," Coyle said.

"Exactly."

Coyle thought Clint would probably react to the chief the same way he did. He wanted to throw the man through the window behind him.

The sheriff stood up.

"All right," he said. "I'll find Adams and talk to him for a while, see what I can find out."

"I'll talk to you later," Blake said.

The sheriff made his way back to the front of the building, where the policeman behind the front desk now ignored him.

He was perfectly willing to talk to Clint Adams, but anything beyond that would be up to the chief and his men. Coyle was too old to start bracing legends now. And he had no deputies to back a play. So talking was as far as he was willing to go.

Maybe it really was time for him to get out of this job.

FIVE

Sheriff Coyle checked a few of the saloons, finally found Clint Adams standing at the bar in The Red Garter.

"Sheriff," Clint said as the man sidled up alongside him. "Hey, I tried that café you told me about."

"How was it?"

"It was great."

"Yeah," Coyle said. "Hannah's the best damn cook in town."

"Then it looks like I found the best place to eat the first time around. Can I buy you a beer?"

"Sure. Why not?"

The bartender brought the lawman a beer with the same bored look on his face.

"You ask Roscoe about your man, Banks?" Coyle asked.

"Roscoe?"

"The bartender."

"No, I hadn't gotten around to it yet."

"Just as well," the sheriff said. "Roscoe's an odd one."

"In what way?"

"He's a bartender who minds his own business."

"Then I guess I wouldn't have gotten much out of him," Clint said. He looked around. "Maybe when the covers come off the tables, I'll find somebody who knows something."

"How long are you willin' to stay in town and look for Banks?" Coyle asked.

"Until I get some answers, I guess," Clint said. "Or until I'm convinced he was never here. Then I'll just have to move on."

"Few days, then."

"Probably," Clint said. "How about the chief of police?"

"I told you," Coyle said. "He's a schoolmaster."

"You said store clerk."

"Same thing," Coyle said. "What I mean is, he's an Easterner. You can go and talk to him if you want, but I gotta warn you. He might not even know who you are."

"That won't be a problem," Clint said. "I don't care if he knows who I am, as long as he knows who Banks is."

Coyle finished his beer and set the empty mug down on the bar.

"Good luck to you, then," he said. "I guess I'll see you around town."

"Sure, Sheriff."

The lawman walked out, watched by Clint and the bartender, Roscoe.

"Another one?" Roscoe asked when Clint looked at him.

"You ever heard of a man named Harlan Banks?" Clint asked.

"Nope."

"Then no," Clint said, "I don't need another one. Thanks."

He decided, instead of waiting for the gaming tables to be opened for business, to move on, try a couple of other saloons, maybe some of the businesses like the mercantile and the hardware stores, places a man might go when he got to town.

He stepped outside the saloon, looked up and down the street. Still busy, with men and women walking back and forth, wagons going up and down the street, as well as horses. In about two hours some of the business would start to close, and the saloons would start to fill up. As dusk came, cowboys from the surrounding ranches would ride in and it would start to get very busy. Clint could have gone to see the chief of police, but he decided to put that off until the next day.

A little saloon hopping first.

SIX

Clint hit two other saloons, engaged the bartenders in some talk, and came up empty. Both men claimed never to have heard of Harlan Banks. Clint thought that was odd. If Banks was in town, he'd be certain to go into several saloons. And he wasn't shy about introducing himself to people.

He decided to stop into one more saloon before going to his room. It was a small place called Brother's Saloon. Inside he found a few men drinking at tables with bored looks on their faces. There was one man at the bar, and as Clint approached, he recognized him. It was Ben, the waiter from Hannah's.

As Clint moved up alongside him, the young man recognized him.

"Hey," Ben said, "fancy meetin' you here. Want a beer?"

"Sure," Clint said, "but aren't you a little young?"

"Actually," Ben said, "I didn't tell ya, but tomorrow's my birthday. I'm twenty-one."

He figured the boy had forgotten he'd already told him he was nineteen, but he decided not to press it.

"In that case, I'll buy." He looked at the bartender and said, "Two beers."

The bartender nodded and delivered them in record time.

"Thank you . . . what did you say your name was?" Ben asked.

"Don't recall if I did, but it's Clint."

"Thanks, Clint."

They both drank.

"So what brings you to Prescott, Clint?" Ben asked.

"I'm looking for somebody," Clint said. "A friend of mine."

"And he's here?"

"I don't know," Clint said. "Either he's here, or he was here."

"What's his name?"

"Harlan Banks," Clint said. "Know him?"

"Banks," Ben said thoughtfully. "No, I don't think I know the name."

"Then I guess if he was here," Clint said, "he didn't manage to find the best restaurant in town."

Ben smiled at that.

"My mom really likes to hear that," he said. "She's worked really hard on the place."

"And what about you?" Clint asked.

"What about me?"

"Well, you're a young man," Clint said. "What have you got planned for your life?"

"I don't know," Ben said with a shrug. "Right now I'm just working with my mom."

"Can you cook?"

"Oh, no," he said, "that's her job. I just wait tables and clean up."

"And that's enough for you?"

"For now," he said. "Hey, I'm only nine—uh, twenty-one."

"Right." Clint looked at the bartender, who was standing there wiping down the bar. "You ever hear of a man named Harlan Banks?"

"Nope," the man said, "can't say I have."

"Yeah," Clint said, "that's the answer I've been getting all over town."

"You talk to the sheriff?" Ben asked.

"I did," Clint said. "He's the one who told me about your restaurant."

"Yeah, he eats there all the time," Ben said. "What about the chief of police?"

"Why? Does he eat there, too?"

"Oh, no," Ben said, "we're too small for him. He eats at some of the fancy places in town. The Red Bull Steakhouse. The dining room in the Magnolia House Hotel. Best food in town—they say."

"Well, no, I haven't talked to the chief yet," Clint said. "I figure to do that in the morning. I heard he's an Easterner."

"Oh, yeah," Ben said, "came here with all kinds of plans to civilize us, turn us into a city."

"As chief of police?"

The bartender, who had been listening, joined in.

"He's got other plans," he said. "Chief of police is just a startin' place for him."

"So he's a politician?"

"Oh, yeah," the barman said. "He's got his sights set on bigger things."

"Like mayor?"

"The mayor's the one who brought him in," the bartender said, "and he's got some plans of his own."

"The mayor wants to move up, and give the chief in his job?"

"That's the way it seems. He's got his eye on the state capital."

"I guess I'll just have to form my own opinion of the man tomorrow."

SEVEN

The door to Clint's cell slammed open.

"Dinnertime," a guard said. The man gestured with his rifle. "Let's go."

Clint stood up from his cot, wiped his hands on the striped pants they'd issued him, along with a matching top.

Once out he wasn't moving fast enough, so the guard prodded him with his rifle.

"Easy," Clint said.

"That's the one thing you don't get in here, Mr. Gunsmith," the guard said. "Don't nothin' come easy in here."

"Nothing comes easy in life, friend."

"You're right about that," the man said, "but it comes a lot harder in here."

The guard was a big, middle-aged man with years of

experience. He had a soft, bulging belly, but his arms and shoulders were still rock-hard muscle.

When Clint got to the prisoners' mess, he joined the line of men waiting to eat. He noticed that at least half of the other prisoners were ignoring him, while the other half turned to look him over. He had known what to expect when he was sent here. Being the Gunsmith without his gun was like having a bull's-eye painted on his back. He was going to be challenged. It was going to happen, and he was as ready for it as he could be. He wondered if it would happen here, during the meal.

Eventually, they reached the point in line where each prisoner could pick up a tray. Everything had to be eaten with spoons, as there were no knives or forks made available to prisoners.

Inside the large mess room, the smell of the cooking food mixed with the odor of unwashed bodies. Clint wondered if he'd be able to eat with just a spoon, but when he saw the gruel that was being served, he knew it didn't matter. There were servers, who scooped the mush into a metal plate and then set a piece of stale or moldy bread on top of it. After that he received a tin cup filled with brackish water.

Clint carried his tray to a table, where several men were already seated, and several more came after him. For the time being the men were giving each other enough elbow room with which to eat. Clint was wondering if his first day would be uneventful. Maybe the prisoners would watch him for a few days before trying something.

Tentatively, he lifted a spoonful of his supper to his nose and sniffed it. That was a bad idea. Next he lifted it to his mouth, took a small bit into his mouth. That was an even worse idea. He quickly took a sip of water, swished it around his mouth. Next he picked up the bread, picked off a few spots of green mold, and bit into it. It was something he thought he'd be able to keep down.

"You gonna eat that?" one prisoner asked him, indicating his tray.

"Huh? Oh, no, help yourself."

Suddenly, hands holding spoons appeared, and everyone at the table got at least one scoop, leaving Clint's plate empty.

The prisoner next to him said, "If you ain't gonna finish that bread, lemme know."

"Sorry," Clint said. "I'm going to eat it."

The man shrugged and went back to his meal.

The prisoner across from Clint said, "After a few days, you'll eat anythin'. Believe me."

"Is it always like this?" Clint asked.

"No, sometimes it's worse," the man said.

Most of the men around him wore either full beards or certain degrees of stubble. This man didn't seem able to sprout anything significant, just a scraggly mustache and a few chin hairs.

"How long have you been here?" Clint asked.

"Six months."

Clint chewed some bread, washed it down with a sip of water.

"Sometimes, if it's a holiday, or the warden's birthday, we'll get a piece of meat."

"Really?"

The man next to him said, "Yeah, but it's greener than the mold on the bread."

"Yeah," somebody else said, "but they cook it so much it don't matter."

"I like burnt meat," still another prisoner said. "At least there ain't nothin' in it that's movin'."

Clint was afraid to ask about breakfast.

Clint did manage to get through the meal without anyone trying to kill him. The same guard walked him back to his cell, which was away from the general population.

The guard pushed him inside, slammed the door, and then stood there looking at him.

"What?" Clint asked.

"Don't think every day, or every meal, is gonna be this easy."

"I didn't think this one would be easy."

"Well," the guard said, "I can help you, if you need help."

"And how much would that cost me?"

"We could come to an understanding."

"And what do I get for my money?"

"Protected."

"From what?"

"From gettin' killed," the guard said. "Sleep on it. If you want me, ask for Ernie."

"Ernie," Clint said. "I'll remember."

But the man he really needed to see was the warden—only not yet.

Ernie tapped his gun barrel on the bars of Clint's cell and said, "Get yerself some sleep. Tomorrow's yer first full day."

Clint sat on his cot, which was almost as unyielding as the floor.

In another cell, two prisoners sat with their heads together, speaking in low tones. Voices carried from cell to cell, and they didn't want anyone else hearing their conversation.

"I know he's the Gunsmith," Chet Barton said, "but in here he's just one of us. He ain't got no gun."

"I know that," his cell mate, Tim Kerry, said. "I just don't wanna rush into anythin'. We don't know who he's aligned with."

"He ain't been here long enough to join with anybody," Barton pointed out.

"Because of who he is, he might already have some people inside."

"And there might be some folks in here who wanna kill him as much as we do."

"That's what I mean," Kerry said. "Let's find out who we got backin' us before we make a move on somebody like him."

"Okay, okay," Barton said, "maybe you're right, but I'm gonna promise you this. Clint Adams ain't gonna walk out of Yuma Prison alive."